Tremor of Demons

Tremor of Demons

FREDERIC LINDSAY

ISIS
LARGE PRINT
Oxford

Copyright © Frederic Lindsay, 2007

First published in Great Britain 2007
by
Allison & Busby Ltd

Published in Large Print 2007 by ISIS Publishing Ltd.,
7 Centremead, Osney Mead, Oxford OX2 0ES
by arrangement with
Allison & Busby Ltd

British Library Cataloguing in Publication Data
Lindsay, Frederic
    Tremor of demons. – Large print ed.
    1. Meldrum, Jim (Fictitious character) – Fiction
    2. Police – Scotland – Edinburgh – Fiction
    3. Mutilation – Fiction
    4. Detective and mystery stories
    5. Large type books
    I. Title
    823.9'14 [F]

ISBN 978–0–7531–7910–9 (hb)
ISBN 978–0–7531–7911–6 (pb)

Printed and bound in Great Britain by
T. J. International Ltd., Padstow, Cornwall

For Catriona

CHAPTER
ONE

In a small hour of the morning, Meldrum, that stolid policeman, had a waking dream in which his wife Carole lay covered in a cloak of bread. He had a notion that he had baked it himself and, having rolled it thin, covered her in a sheet of it from throat to thighs. When he put his lips on it, the bread smelled fresh and wholesome and the delicate fabric of it softened under his tongue until he could suck on her right nipple, the one nearest to the side on which he had been sleeping. He wondered then about going down between her legs, but he was six foot four and on a winter's night it didn't seem a good idea to have his legs sprawl out from under the warmth of the blanket. It was also the case, he reflected lazily, that it wasn't something they had often done. In fact, he thought of it as an American obsession and had always wondered if men there had a problem with keeping an erection. In a book of poems given to him by an old man who had later been murdered, he'd found the image of a woman's body as a country and just then that was how Carole seemed to him: a landscape of hills and a fertile plain and a junction like the secret inwardness of a fjord. It was natural to compare a woman who was loved to a place

1

that was loved, though once he'd met an MP who had been an advocate of using a site in Caithness in the North East as a dump for nuclear waste. In any country other than Scotland, the man would have been bribed and worked in darkness, hiding his corruption from the light. This was an honest man, however, no need to waste money on bribing him, arguing his case to anyone who would listen, and one who was re-elected time after time after time. How could that be? What was missing, in the man, in the country? What had happened?

Thinking about the strangeness of it, he must have slept. Just for an instant as he opened his eyes, he smelled the warmth of freshly baked bread, but the place beside him was cold. Carole and he had been separated for years, and she lay now beside a new husband in a bed on the other side of the city; and, as for his country, he had wakened to a grey drained light and a roaring of wind as it battered rain against the glass.

CHAPTER
TWO

A dead man who has lain undiscovered for some weeks smells nothing like fresh bread. Even in life, this body might have offended the nose, since the corpse was of a fat old man and the house, though well enough furnished, seemed none too clean.

The young constable who had found the body was pallid with a light sweat showing on her forehead and cheeks. When Meldrum arrived, he'd been annoyed to find she was still in the front room, staring at the corpse as if hypnotised. He'd taken her out through the hall and on to the common landing.

Staring at the stripes of dust picked out by the sun on the landing window, he asked her, "Sharon, isn't it?"

"Sharon Nisbet, Sir."

"And you found him?" He watched muscles slither under the skin of her throat as she swallowed. "The first is always the worst."

"It wasn't my first, sir." When he raised his eyebrows, she explained, "Just after I left College, I had to go to the morgue. We all had to do it. I didn't want to, I couldn't sleep for a week. I tried to make an excuse, but the big sergeant told me it had to be done. He said, one day you'll lift a letter box and know by the smell there's a body inside."

"Which is what happened?"

"His neighbour was worried. She hadn't seen him for weeks. We broke in and he was lying there in the middle of the floor. Just as if he'd been going to make himself a cup of tea and fallen over. Something sudden like a heart attack."

"But?" Meldrum knew there had to be a reason for suspicion.

"It was his slippers, sir. They were on the wrong feet."

"And who noticed that?"

McGuigan, Meldrum's DS came out of the flat in time to hear her answer.

"So you were the one," he said.

The girl cleared her throat and her cheeks reddened. With his boxer's physique and dark good looks, McGuigan had that effect on a lot of women.

"I just happened to notice," she said modestly.

The sergeant's look of scorn suggested he hadn't intended a compliment. "Don't know how you managed that," he said. "They're so old and bashed about probably wouldn't matter which way they went on."

When Meldrum went back into the house, he found Dr Fleming, ruddy cheeked and thick set, peeling the gloves from his hands as he rose from beside the body.

"Nothing to say it wasn't a natural death," he offered.

"Hard to tell after so long," Meldrum said.

4

"Aye, he'll bubble when we cut him. I'll let you know once I've had a proper look, but at the moment nothing."

"So far so good then."

"You've enough on your plate, eh?"

Meldrum nodded, his eyes on the carpet slippers on the corpse's feet. The flies were crawling across them. A smell to sicken a slaughterman, and Fleming and him chatting on either side of the body. What's happened to us? he thought. The slippers were very old, soft and crumpled; what his mother would have called "baffies". It seemed likely the old man could have worn them wrong way round without discomfort.

Following his glance, the doctor smiled. With a nod at McGuigan, who was talking to the second constable who'd broken in to find the body, he said, "Your sergeant wasn't amused at the girl playing detective."

"Was he not?" Meldrum asked drily.

"But then," the doctor speculated, "I doubt he laughs a lot." He laughed himself, and shook his head at Meldrum. "The two of you are well matched."

CHAPTER
THREE

The first disciple had been given the name Cadoc. As a matter of security that was how he was referred to always within the group. With the other three it was the same and, with practice, they had broken themselves — when the Convenor was there — of the habit of using their real names.

He woke up reluctantly that morning, and lay for what felt like a long time with his eyes closed. When the alarm rang, he would have to get up. Get up at once and without hesitation. That was part of their training for what was to come. It was just that he knew this was the morning of a difficult day, one that he was dreading. He despised his own weakness, but he couldn't help it. He had done harder things than today would demand of him. He told himself that, and stretched out, hands by his sides, feeling his face tighten around the clenching of his eyes. As he lay, he pictured the clock that sat on a wooden chair in the middle of the room. A cheap clock, bought for the purpose when it was decided they should all sleep in the same room, with a round face and big numbers like something made to help children tell the time. It wasn't electric but had to be wound up every night to make sure that it would go off in the morning. Since he was the only man in the flat, that had been appointed as one of his tasks. Right now the hands would be moving to mark the hour of six. He imagined he could see them and counted down till the alarm went off, got it wrong and was half way through a second count when it rattled out its summons.

In a moment, he was standing beside his bed. Already the other three were up and ready. Although they weren't allowed heating in the flat, no one was shivering. There was a late summer leniency in the air and the warmth of their bodies had heated the room during the night.

After the usual rituals and a bus journey across town, he went with dragging steps into the shop. As a student, he'd worked at a variety of weekend and holiday jobs. He'd even worked for a month in a shop not unlike this one and not minded it too much. The difference was that he had graduated since then, and entered a profession and obtained a different image of himself. Perhaps that was why he had been told to take the job here, a job he hadn't applied for, somehow he had been given it, somehow it had been arranged, and so he would come here every morning until he was told it was over. Perhaps he had been too proud?

It felt as if the shopkeeper and the fat girl took pleasure in mocking his clumsiness and his mistakes until the long day ended with the man pressing some notes into his hand and sneering, "You needn't come back. Haven't you classes to take?"

In consolation, all day he gave no thought to the old man and the noise he had made as he died.

CHAPTER
FOUR

Among the depressed, the bereaved and the lonely, suicide peaks at Christmas. Since New Year means more to Scots than other people, Hogmanay too is bad for self harm. This August, Meldrum added the annual Festival to such low points of the year. He went about his business doing his best to ignore the crowded streets, the grinning young people thrusting handfuls of playbills on passersby, the clowns and jugglers performing on the steps of the National Gallery. He wasn't in a mood for celebration.

When he found the house, he was surprised to find it so large. Education must pay well, he thought sourly. His ex-wife had married an educational administrator, who had moved from local government into one of the universities. The city had three or four of them, it wasn't easy to keep count, and he had no idea which one Don Corrigan graced with his oily charms.

When Carole opened the door, she stared in surprise.

"I thought you were coming last night," she said.

"The job. You know."

Of course, she did. The demands of the job more than any other factor had brought about the breakdown of their marriage.

"You might have phoned."

No point in saying he'd been too busy. He could have found a moment, if he'd remembered. The demands of the job; some people kept them in check; for others like himself they were all absorbing.

In silence, he followed her inside. She led the way into the front room. Automatically he took in the surroundings, heavy arm chairs with bulging arms, polished floor with white rugs, pictures on the walls, the one above the fireplace of skyscrapers reflected in shaky swirls of bright colour in the water of a harbour.

"How is she?" he asked.

"She's coping. Just about."

They were speaking softly, the same tones it struck him they would have used in discussing an invalid.

"I'd like to speak to her," he said.

"You should have come before. She's been out of hospital for weeks."

"I think about her a lot." All the time, in fact; and he'd met her several times in town, but promised not to say.

"Anyway, she's out this evening."

He stared in something like outrage.

Before he could say anything, Carole went on, "She has a meeting with her therapist. It should have been last night, but she got it moved."

If it had been so that she could see him, he hadn't turned up. Maybe if he'd phoned, Betty could have gone to the therapist last night and been here this evening. When she was a child and her mother needed him he had never been there, and now it was the same pattern. Nothing changed, it seemed. The demands of the job. University administrators no doubt kept office hours.

"Don's been wonderful with Tommy," Carole said. It was as if she had read his mind. She'd always been good at that.

"Can I see the boy?" When she seemed to hesitate, he said sharply, "I am his grandfather."

"How long is it since you saw him?"

"I think," Meldrum said bitterly, "he'll still recognise me. I'm the only grandpa he's got."

Maybe, he thought, Betty's ex-husband Sandy wouldn't have broken up his marriage if his father had still been alive. Some sons didn't kick over the traces until their father died. Two live grandfathers might have made all the difference for wee Tommy.

"He's in bed," Carole said. "I'll see if he's still awake."

When she came back, she led him upstairs, but stopped and pointed at a door instead of taking him in.

There was only a bedside lamp on, gathering two figures into its pool of light.

Meldrum said, "Hello, wee man."

"Hello, Grandpa," the boy said. In the shadowy light, he looked like his father and even more like his big brother, the one who had died.

Don Corrigan laid the book he was holding face down on the bed. "I try always to be here to read a story to the little chap at bedtime. He'd like it finished. If that's all right with you?"

Thinking it must have only a little to go, Meldrum shrugged and took a seat on the other side of the bed.

"It's called," said Corrigan, "*The Three Brothers and the Magic Axe.*"

Twenty minutes later Meldrum was sure the boy was asleep but Corrigan kept on reading. He didn't stop even when Meldrum grunted, though his voice faltered when the big man stood up.

Carole was standing in the hall as he came down the stairs.

"Is everything all right?"

She sounded anxious. Her face was thinner than he remembered.

The anger went out of him and he said softly, "Everything's fine."

She relaxed. "You were so long."

And he couldn't stop himself from saying, "I was listening to a bedtime story."

Her eyes flickered and went past him as if to see if someone else was coming down to join them.

After a pause, she said, "Tommy's been upset. A story helps him to sleep."

"The Magic Axe," Meldrum said. "One brother cut off his arm with it. The other cut off his leg. But the third brother cut off his head. He was the one who got the treasure."

"Children need stories like that. It helps them to deal with anxiety. There's so much they don't understand."

12

At one time, when they were married, she'd run a primary school. He didn't argue with her; no doubt there would be research to prove she was right. He decided against telling her that he hadn't been there the previous night because he had been at a murder. Four blows to the head with an axe. "It belonged tae my uncle," the teenage son had said, the sleeve of his jacket red with blood. "He was in the fire brigade, ken, and he kept it when he left." The last blow had been so hard that it had split the skull between the victim's eyes.

"You could be right," Meldrum said. "Do you know the story?" She shook her head.

"He claimed to be reading it. A hell of a long story. Maybe he was making it up as he went along."

CHAPTER
FIVE

Being tethered to his mobile had made it easy for Meldrum to be contacted. Still half asleep, he reached for it without opening his eyes. As he did, he touched the naked breasts of the woman beside him. The phone wasn't where it usually was, laid on the table beside his bed, but then he realised more or less at once that the bed he was in wasn't his.

As he listened to the phone, the woman sat up and yawned. She was in her thirties with a tangle of long blonde hair. Heavy make up round her eyes gave her a startled look. He answered McGuigan with a series of monosyllables that ended with a promise to meet him "there", meaning the morgue, closed the phone and swung his feet out of bed. He found his clothes on a chair, neatly folded though he had no memory of putting them there. As he dressed, he remembered the previous night, leaving Carole's house, going into the bar of a hotel. He remembered drinking. He didn't remember meeting the woman.

Putting on his shoes, he asked, "Did I pay you?"

"Oh, aye. I mean, there isn't a problem, is there?"

"No problem."

"If you want the money, you can have it back."

He looked at her. "Why would you do that?"

"You gave me it. I mean, I wasn't asking for it."

"Fuck," he said. "You know who I am, don't you?"

She thought about that, rubbing her hands slowly over her breasts. It was cold in the room and her nipples brushed back and forward as she rubbed. At last, she shook her head. ". . . No. I don't know who you are. Honest."

"Aye, right," he said in disbelief. It was a long time since he had wakened up in a prostitute's bed. Angry at his own stupidity, he said menacingly, "Just keep your mouth shut. If I hear you've been flapping your mouth about me, you'll be sorry."

Her look of fright disgusted him with himself.

"Forget it," he said. "It doesn't matter." No wife to distress. Not a chance in a million of anyone taking a whore's word against his. Why should it matter? Fuck it. "If you knew who I was, why did you go with me?"

"You asked," she said with a grin. After a hesitation, she added, "You were nice last night," she said. "Not like some."

"I don't do favours," he said.

He put on his jacket and slipped the phone into its zipped inside pocket.

Behind him, she said, "You told me about your daughter. About her man leaving her."

"You talk too much," he said. "In your job, it doesnae do to talk too much."

"Sorry." She let the word out on a little gasping breath, as if it was one she often needed to use.

". . . You could have a cup of tea before you go. And I've got rolls."

He looked at her and shook his head.

As he was opening the door, she said, "I'm Marie. You'll know where to find me."

Although, with luck, he'd never see her again, policeman's habit meant that as he walked blinking in the sunlight out from the close in the street behind Tollcross he automatically took note of the number.

CHAPTER
SIX

Dr Fleming had been right. The corpse had bubbled with maggots at the first cut into the chest. Meldrum regarded himself as fortunate for not having been there, and didn't relish Fleming's blow-by-blow description. What mattered was the evidence that the death in the flat the previous day had not been from natural causes. The news didn't come entirely as a surprise. For no reason that Meldrum could put his finger on, the death of the old man had nagged at him.

"It would have been easy to miss," Fleming said with satisfaction. "The state of the body meant that there was no way of making sure it really was a flesh wound. But when I peeled back to the bone to make sure, there it was. Just above the hairline." He was referring to a puncture punched through the bone at the base of the skull. "Through the cerebellum and up into the brain. Death would have been instantaneous. No way it could be accidental. Whoever did it was either knowledgeable or had been shown what to do. The old fellow — what was his name?"

Meldrum's mind went blank. "Michael Thorne," McGuigan volunteered. The memory man. Clever bastard.

"Right. No doubt about it, Mr Thorne was murdered."

Meldrum sighed at the word. "You did a good job spotting it," he said grudgingly.

"There was the clue of the slippers on the wrong feet."

Fleming spoke with mock solemnity, then laughed at McGuigan.

McGuigan stared at him. "That sounds like a clue you might have noticed yesterday," he said unsmilingly.

A wave of tiredness washed over Meldrum.

"Anything else?" he forced himself to ask.

"I'll let you have what I can work out about the thickness and length of the blade. At the moment, think of something like an ice pick."

"An ice pick?" McGuigan asked. "He's seen too many old gangster films," he said to Meldrum, giving Fleming a sour glance. "Do they even make them any more?"

"Something like one then." Fleming shrugged and laughed. "And one more thing. He'd three long red hairs caught in his fist. A woman's by the look of them. Would you call that a clue, sergeant? They've gone to forensics."

"What now?" McGuigan asked, as they left the building.

"Put a team together. Door to door round the neighbours."

"And there's the son," McGuigan said, his tone carefully casual.

"What son?" What fucking son?

"After Fleming phoned, I checked with the boys in blue. They traced a son. Works at the university. They got him there and told him his father had been found dead." He paused. "Took it pretty calmly, apparently. Too calmly, one of the woolly suits thought."

CHAPTER
SEVEN

As they walked along the corridor, Meldrum said, "So the lassie was right after all."

"What?"

"The wee police constable. She was right about the slippers. It was murder." He tried to remember her name. Sharon something. "A good head on her shoulders, she could go far."

"She got lucky," McGuigan said, curling his lip.

The sergeant wasn't fond of hearing anyone else praised. Not only smart, but ambitious. Sometimes, though, the smartest thing was to hide how ambitious you were. Meldrum gave him a smile that to a casual glance might have seemed friendly. McGuigan looked away.

"There we are. Beginning to think they'd sent us the wrong way. That's his name on the door."

A hand written note pinned to the door was signed: COLIN HALLIDAY.

As Meldrum raised a hand to knock, the door opened and three young people came into the corridor. A slim man in his late twenties followed them, clutching a sheaf of papers in his left hand.

"Till next week," he told the group, all of them watching the two strangers as they milled past into the corridor.

"Mr Halliday?" Meldrum asked.

Waiting until the students had moved off, Halliday asked with a frown, "Police?" and as they confirmed this, he added, "I've been told about my father."

"It would be better if we could have a word in private," Meldrum said.

"You'd better come in here then."

He led them into the room he'd just left. A blackboard that had been wiped clean in swirls of smeared chalk, a small table, a group of chairs arranged in a half circle. "I've just finished a seminar. No one else should be in for a bit." He took his place behind the table, leaning his hands on it. "*Detective* Inspector." He stressed the word as if just taking it in. "I can't imagine why you're here. The constable who told me about my father asked when I last saw him. I'll tell you what I told him. My father was a difficult man. We didn't get on terribly well. He left us when I was ten. My mother remarried and I took my stepfather's name." He looked from one face to the other. Not finding perhaps what he searched for, he went on, "I'm sorry, of course, that his body lay for so long, if that's what this is about. But I can't see any point in your being here."

"There's been a change since yesterday," Meldrum said. "We've discovered how your father died." And when the young man raised his eyebrows, went on, "His skull was punctured with some kind of instrument.

We're told death must have been instantaneous. It's not the kind of injury that could have been self-inflicted."

Halliday sat down slowly as if controlling his decline. After a moment, he asked, "Are you saying it was an accident?"

"Your father was found lying on the floor of his kitchen. There wasn't any obvious sign of an attack — or anything that could have been used as a weapon." Again Halliday kept silent as if waiting for something more. After a moment, Meldrum added, "That's why the medical examiner thought it was a natural death. But when he conducted a proper examination, he found the wound." In illustration, he turned his head and laid the tip of a finger to the base of his skull.

"Natural?" Halliday asked. "How could he have thought it was natural? I mean, if there was a wound there must have been blood? Didn't he see blood?"

"He didn't, I didn't. Somebody must have wiped the floor. And the hair at the back of his head. Even a careful look wouldn't have spotted blood. Anyway, I understand that there wouldn't have been much."

"All the same, I'm not impressed."

"The body had been there for days. It wasn't in a good state."

As he spoke, it struck him the son of a victim deserved more sympathetic handling. It wasn't an excuse that the overhead light put a halo round the cropped blond hair; or that he looked so clean his skin seemed to shine. Truth was Meldrum had reacted to him as a young man with an expensive look about him holding down a soft indoor job. A member of the pampered middle class. This despite the dead old man, shabbily dressed, lying in a sparsely furnished flat that was none too clean. Anyway, to Meldrum's eye the son was a touch too unruffled for a man who had just learned his father had been murdered. Even an estranged father.

"I've just been conducting a seminar on the problem of evil," Halliday said. "My father would have appreciated that."

Was that the faintest trace of a smile on his lips?

"Why would that be?" McGuigan asked. The abruptness of the question suggested that something about Halliday was grating on him as well.

"Appreciated the coincidence, I mean." And when they looked at him blankly, this time he gave a full smile as he explained, "That I should be talking about evil when you come to tell me he has been murdered. You do know that my father was a minister?"

"No," Meldrum said.

We don't know anything about him, he almost said, but we'll have to find out now. A kind of weariness filled him at the thought. The process unfolded ahead of him as it had done so often before.

"Oh, yes," the young man said. "In the Pentecostal church." He frowned as if in embarrassment. "But he's been retired, of course, for a long time."

"Am I right in thinking you weren't in close contact with him?"

Halliday gave a little nod.

"When did you last see him?"

"Months ago. February perhaps. I don't really remember. It was a vile day. Very wet. I didn't stay long."

"And before that?"

"I called in just after the New Year. Took him a bottle of whisky." He shook his head. "I don't drink myself. Since he didn't open it there and then, I'm not sure whether he did at all. Perhaps he gave it away."

"Are you his only family?" Meldrum asked.

"Yes."

"I take it your mother is dead?"

Halliday stared. "What on earth makes you think that?"

"You mean she isn't?"

"Of course not."

"I'd be grateful if you would let us have her name and an address where she could be contacted."

"Why would you want that?" He sounded genuinely puzzled. Before Meldrum could respond, he continued, "As I said, they've been separated for years. Since I was ten. She won't be able to tell you anything."

"All the same."

Halliday shrugged and began to scribble on a sheet of paper. Upside down, it seemed to be a name with an address underneath.

As they waited, McGuigan chipped in. "Did she keep in touch with your father?"

Without looking up, Halliday said, "If she did, I'd be surprised. It wasn't that kind of break up. There was another woman involved." He lifted his head and studied McGuigan for a moment. He gave the impression of weighing up a student out of his depth. "My father wasn't cut out for marriage."

"Can you tell us who your father's friends were?" Meldrum intervened, only to be favoured with the same slow look of dismissal.

"To the best of my knowledge, he hadn't any."

Thinking of the bare austerity of the flat in which the body had lain, Meldrum tried to remember if he had seen a television or any sign of books.

"Do you know anything about how he occupied his time?"

"I can't think of any hobbies, if that's what you mean," Halliday said. He smiled. "And certainly he'd no women friends, so you can rule out that as a way of filling his time."

CHAPTER
EIGHT

The youngest disciple, Emer, was only nineteen. Though the undemanding nature of the course she was following meant there was no external measure by which to compare her to the others, some intrinsic quality in her blue eyes and the broad forehead, skin like milk under the vibrant red of her hair, seemed to offer a promise that she might be the most intelligent of the four. Certainly, numbers of young men had found her so sympathetic a listener they had been in no doubt that she must be clever.

At least it could be said that apart from any need to study, she read for pleasure. The morning after the first execution, she had gone out as if to her classes, but then, unable to face some preening lecturer taking sly glances at her breasts, had sneaked back into the flat. Taking up a book of Chekhov stories at the point she had laid it down the day before, she found this passage and read it as she rested one hand on the warm mound between her legs:

"Likharayov's face darkened. 'And I'll tell you, women have always been and will always be slaves to men,' he said in his bass voice, striking the table with his fist. 'A woman is a soft, delicate piece of wax from which man will make whatever he wants. Goodness me, for a man's worthless passion a woman will be ready to cut her hair off, abandon her family, and die abroad . . . And among the ideas for which she will sacrifice herself there will not be one that she can call her own! She will be a selfless, devoted slave! I have not measured skulls, but I'm telling you this on the basis of my own hard and bitter experience. If I have managed to inspire them, the proudest and most independent women have followed me without a moment's thought, asking no questions and doing everything I have wanted; there was a nun who I turned into a nihilist, who I later heard went and shot a policeman; my wife never left me in my wanderings for a minute, and changed her faith like a weather-vane whenever I changed mine.'"

She laid the book down on her knee and stared sightlessly at the lozenge of sunlight on the kitchen wall opposite the window. The passage seemed to describe her situation exactly, but knowing it was so made no difference. It seemed that a thing was so and having understanding of it, even insight into it, did not unmake its effect on her.

Until the worst happened, however, there had been a doubt at the heart of her submission, like a flaw in a precious stone. Until she saw the old man die, she hadn't been sure, not certain into the deepest recess of her soul. But with his death she understood in the bright morning that all her doubts were gone. Apprehending the suck as the narrow blade was drawn out of the clasp of the skull, seeing the drops of red blood, hearing his sigh as life left him, how could what they had done not be about saving the world?

CHAPTER
NINE

Detectives had talked to all the old man's neighbours, and come up blank in every case. There was no gossip, no word of a quarrel, no real knowledge of who he was or what kind of man he had been. He had lived in the flat for almost ten years, but it was as if Michael Thorne had gone to earth like an animal determined to keep the world at bay. To Meldrum's surprise, none of the neighbours even knew what his job had been before he retired.

"A minister?" Calum Grant said. "A man of the cloth? You really do *surprise* me."

It was that note of animus that had made his an interview Meldrum thought might be worth following up in person.

"Why would that be?"

Grant was a pale wrinkled man somewhere around seventy years of age. In the middle of the morning, he was still in his dressing gown and slippers. His first reaction at the sight of the two large men on his doorstep had been to take a step back ready to retreat inside as quickly as possible. Once reassured, he perched on the edge of a chair and said with the slow emphasis of a man sharing a valuable insight, "He was unsociable."

"Unsociable?"

"Correct me if I'm wrong, but I always assumed that would be one of the qualifications for the job. Wouldn't you think a clergyman of any kind would be interested in people? At the least, you'd be surprised if he didn't like them."

"Mr Thorne didn't like people?"

"He didn't."

"Your other neighbours only describe him as someone who kept himself to himself."

Grant sniffed. "*All* of them do. But it was more than that with him. I should know, I made an effort to get to know him. More than any of them would ever do. He came to live downstairs about ten years ago. I'd lost my wife two years before that. I'd — what's the phrase you used? — been keeping myself to myself. Two years for mourning, anyone ever tell you that's the time it takes to get over a death? I wasn't over my wife's death, but I'd have welcomed a bit of company. I made some overtures. It made sense. Two widowers, why not share the loneliness? He was damned rude."

"Widower?" McGuigan asked. "His ex-wife's still alive. At least according to his son."

"Oh God, I'd just assumed — that makes it even worse. I was speaking to him about my dead wife. Got a little emotional, I'm afraid. It was too early for such a conversation, but I'd been bottling it up for a long time. I'd met him on the stairs. In retrospect, I can't imagine why he accepted my invitation to come in for a cup of tea. He sat in that chair there and hardly said a word. And I found myself talking about Netta. He didn't sympathise, nothing like that, but there was something in the way he listened that made me go on."

"If he was a minister," Meldrum said, "he must have heard a lot of talk about death."

". . . I suppose. But he certainly didn't offer a word of sympathy. If you're going down that line, wouldn't you expect him to have a few phrases to hand, however little he might have meant them? No, he just sat. And I went on and on. Silence implies consent kind of thing, I suppose. Makes me embarrassed to think of it, even now. Makes me angry, to be honest." He pursed his thin lips. "Anyway, when he did say something it was about himself."

He paused long enough to make McGuigan, never a patient man, repeat, "About himself?"

"Hmm. He said, I had someone I cared for like that — I still think about her. His wife, I thought, dead like my poor Netta. What else would I think? I asked him his wife's name. Aileen, he said. I was ridiculously pleased to have him share that with me. I was ready, you see, to set out on the path of friendship. Two grieving old men. Then he said, But the woman I was talking about was called Bridget. And he started laughing. A sound like a gate creaking. At a guess, laughing wasn't something he did often." The thin lips twisted. "I've never cared less for a man. But then he had made a fool of me, and no one cares for that."

CHAPTER
TEN

The flat in which the old man died had been taken apart, photographed, and searched for fingerprints, stains of blood or mucus. All the neighbours had been interviewed, some more than once, each time only reinforcing the impression of how little any of them had spoken to Michael Thorne in the ten years they had all lived under the same roof. On his part, it seemed, human contact had been kept to a minimum. Even the woman who had called the police had done so less from concern than curiosity. "I'd see him in the morning quite often, going out to get his paper, I suppose," she'd said, "and then a fortnight ago I realised I hadn't, not for some time. When I thought of that, I knocked on his door. I did that for a week on and off. And then when my sister visited and I told her, she said, 'Something's wrong!'"

There had been no sighting of a stranger in the building on the day of the murder, and none of the neighbours, not even the acerbic Calum Grant, made for a plausible suspect.

Just before the morning conference, Meldrum had an idea.

"Am I right in thinking there wasn't any food in the flat?" he asked the assembled detectives.

"Milk in the fridge," Houston said.

"Coffee? He'd coffee in a jar. Can't remember tea."

"There was tea in a canister."

"Right," Meldrum said. "No bread, no eggs, no porridge or muesli or cheese."

"He ate out," McGuigan said, as if pointing out the obvious.

"Houston and MacIntosh and Sharkey. Check the pubs and cafés round about."

"How far out do you want us to check?" Houston asked.

"Till you get a result."

"Maybe," McGuigan said, grinning at them, "he liked a walk before breakfast."

Not a long one fortunately. The women behind the counter in the nearest café recognised the photograph. It had been lying in a drawer in the dead man's bedroom, a ragged line indicating where it had been torn to leave him uncompanioned, and had been computer modified by some forty years into a good resemblance of the old man. Every weekday morning, Sharkey had been told, Thorne had eaten a bacon roll and drunk a cup of tea. "Came in about ten. Never missed." Whatever need he satisfied by having people around him while he ate, it hadn't been for conversation. "Never got a word out of him. With him being so regular, some of us tried — you know since he was always on his own. He was quite rude to May. Can't remember what he said exactly, I mean this was years ago, but she was offended. After that, he came in and ate and went off again. He didn't speak, and none of us felt like trying. Not after he'd been rude. Every morning the same. We were always glad to see the back of him."

Later that day, Meldrum went to the building where Michael Thorne had been killed. When he got there, he realised that he had brought the key of the flat but not one to open the outer door. He pressed buttons on the entry board by the door until someone buzzed it open. Instead of taking the lift, he went up by the stairs, taking them two at a time until he got to the fire door on the fourth floor. The round overhead lights shone down on the blue carpet of the corridor. He went past two doors and round the corner into the short stretch that ended at Thorne's door. Looking back, he saw someone had put a bowl of plants under the window set in the corner. It was a nice building, not more than twenty years old, and most of the occupants were retired or not far from doing so. Some had come back from abroad and others had sold houses to release capital; a few had bought one of the flats as an investment and rented it out. He decided that it would be worth asking the son Colin whether his father had bought the flat and, if so, where he had found the money. Going by the furniture and the life the old man had been leading, money had been in short supply.

He stripped the tape off the door, and stood with a piece of it in his hand. After a moment, he dropped it on the carpet and went inside. He had made a point of going alone, and when he had let himself in conducted no kind of organised search since that had already been expertly done. Instead he drifted from one room to the other. In the kitchen, he opened the fridge and looked at the empty shelves, opened a cupboard door and found nothing more interesting than a pot of jam half eaten with a stained spoon balanced on top of it. He went into the bedroom and, leaning down, pressed with both hands on the bed. The mattress was brick hard. He ran the back of his hand along the coverlet and was struck by the contrast of how smooth and soft it felt. Lifting a corner he rubbed his cheek against the cloth, imagining how it must have felt to the old man stretched out between it and the unforgiving mattress. In the living room, he sat in the single armchair and looked around him. Rather than the lack of comfort, he was most struck by the absence of any kind of way of passing time. There was no sign of the ubiquitous television set, no radio, no books. Looking at the wall, alone with his thoughts, how had Thorne put in his evenings?

Out in the street again, Meldrum walked along to the café on the corner. He thought about going in, but watching through the window the elderly waitress serving tea and scones to a group of what must be patients from some nearby Home, he shook his head and turned away. Sharkey had found whatever was to be found about Thorne's solitary breakfasts. He started off down Morningside Road in the direction of the café where Thorne had made a practice of taking his lunch. According to Houston's report, the story there hadn't been much different: the same unvarying routine:

arriving about midday, drinking coffee instead of tea, taking a baguette.

He took his time. If he'd been asked, he might have excused his sauntering pace by claiming to be double checking in case the detectives had missed somewhere in which Thorne might have eaten dinner. It seemed certain that he had eaten that meal too out of his flat. It was possible that the later meal might throw up something more interesting than lunch and breakfast had. All of which was true, but it was also true that he needed time on his own. The sun slanted down the hill and as he went he glanced into the side streets, turning off once to show the photograph in a pub only to be told others had been there before him.

He was almost at Tollcross before he spotted the lunch place on the corner of the main street and one leading into the Meadows. It was small but looked comfortable with low couches in front of two long tables. There was another table by the window with a scatter of free papers. It was empty except for a pretty young woman in jeans collecting cups. Why not? he thought, and went in.

When the woman brought a coffee over to the couch, he showed her the photograph.

"But I've already been through this with the chap who was here already."

"Detective Constable Houston, right?"

"Are you his boss?"

"That's right."

"Was there something he forgot to ask?"

"Would you mind just confirming what you told him?"

She went through it again, affirming the old man's regularity, the routine of his arrival, the repetition in what he ate. "He didn't seem to care about his food. Never showed any sign of enjoying it." She smiled. "But he kept coming back."

"A regular customer."

"You could say that. Maybe it was the papers. Some days, he seemed to find something interesting and he'd take a second coffee." She paused, and then said, as if on impulse, "I could have done without him. But you can't bar somebody just for making you feel uneasy."

"In what way?"

She frowned as if trying to find the right words. "Sometimes I'd catch him looking at me. Nothing obvious, nothing you could object to. I could just feel his eyes on me sometimes. Not very often — most of the time it was if he was avoiding even a glance. Maybe that was it. He gave me this feeling he didn't want to look — that he was really struggling against it — and then it would happen. As if he couldn't help himself." She laughed in embarrassment. "I don't mean because it was *me*."

"You're a good looking girl," Meldrum said, and catching her frown wondered if she objected to being called a girl. Good looking woman, then, he thought.

"It was about him, not me. Do you know what I mean?"

"I think so."

"That's how I felt. I didn't say that before. To your detective constable. You're a good listener."

"Nice to know."

She smiled. "Mind you, he came in earlier and I was busy."

Just then the door opened and two women came in. As they were standing at the counter looking at the display of cakes, Meldrum got up to leave.

"Thanks for your help," he said.

"Something's happened to the old man, hasn't it? The policeman earlier wouldn't say."

"No secret," Meldrum said. "He's dead."

CHAPTER
ELEVEN

Half way along Melville Drive, the car pulled up alongside him. "You're easy to spot," McGuigan said, opening the passenger door. "One benefit of being tall." Putting the car in gear, he asked, "You didn't say where you wanted to go?"

"Mobile phone," Meldrum grunted. He believed it was best to keep conversation on a mobile to a minimum for fear of frying your brains. It was a theory he'd explained to an unconvinced McGuigan.

"So where to?"

"Turn right now."

"Marchmont Road. Didn't Colin Halliday give an address there?"

"For his mother," Meldrum confirmed. A moment later, he said, "Anywhere here would do."

A moment later they were stopped. McGuigan was one of those drivers who could conjure a parking space out of nothing. They started back down the hill, but had gone only half a block when Meldrum spotted the number of the close where Halliday claimed his mother lived.

As they climbed the stair, McGuigan wondered, "I take it you phoned?" And getting no answer, couldn't keep an edge of irritation out of the speculation, "Bit of a waste of time, if she's not in."

Since he hadn't phoned and it would be self evidently a waste of time, Meldrum scowled and said nothing. On the third floor, he hit the bell and waited. Time passed and he was conscious of McGuigan's sidelong look of disgusted disbelief.

He was pleased when the door finally opened.

The woman was neat and slightly built and her hair was black. For the ex-wife of a dead 73-year-old, she looked in good condition.

"Mrs Halliday?"

"You must be the police," she said.

Introductions over and seated inside the living room, high-ceilinged, smelling of furniture polish despite every surface being littered with magazines, she explained, "My son described you both to me. He lives nearby, did you know that? He wouldn't have it any other way. His father left when he was ten and from then on he felt it was his job to look after me."

There was a long oak sideboard with photographs facing the chair Meldrum had been assigned. Over her shoulder, he saw the largest photograph showed a plump white haired man with his arm around Mrs Halliday. Whoever he was, it wasn't Michael Thorne.

She turned to follow the direction of his glance, and said, "That's my late husband."

"Mr Halliday?"

"Yes. So sad."

"He's dead?"

Her expression remained serene as turning again, she said, "He went off with my sister. It came as a surprise, but I don't envy her. I don't envy her at all. He's a man who promises more than he can deliver."

Plenty of those around, Meldrum thought, not excepting himself. It wasn't something he would be expected to say, though, so he let the thought sink in his mind and asked, "Did your son tell you about your first husband's death?" He added, "Michael Thorne."

"Why did you give his name?" She looked at him and widened her eyes. "Was it in case I'd had more than two husbands?"

When he hesitated, she gave a little smile. "It isn't impossible. If I had, he'd probably have left as well as the others. I haven't been lucky with husbands. But no, just the two." She glanced from one man to the other. "At least, for the moment. I'm not sixty yet. I suppose I could marry again."

Trying to get the conversation back on track, Meldrum tried once more. "So you know what happened?"

"That he was murdered?"

Meldrum nodded.

"I'll tell you what I told Colin. I haven't spoken to his father in years. And it turns out he was living in Edinburgh! I might have passed him in the street without noticing! Seventy-three! He was only forty-something when I married him. It was a time when I had been very unhappy. No point in asking me why! It was about a man, of course. Charlie his name was, but I've bother even picturing his face now. He meant enough to me then that I'd had a breakdown. The day I went to Michael's church I could taste iron in my mouth. Electric shock has that effect on some people. After his sermon, I stood up and started to give my confession — but as he explained later I wasn't using English. Speaking in tongues, they call it. I was a different person then. The day before he and I got married, I heard Jesus on the bus. I can't tell you what He said, not now, it's a long time ago. But I remember the number of the bus. It was a 44, going to Musselburgh!"

Meldrum opened his mouth and closed it again. He glanced at McGuigan and saw a look of something that was almost fright. As a devout man, the sergeant might be superstitious about blasphemy and bolts of lightning, or perhaps he was wondering how sane she was. Maybe he preferred confessions that had to be wrung out rather than bursting out like oil gushing from the earth.

He looked back at Mrs Halliday just in time to catch her throwing back her head as she laughed. "I'm just telling you about the past," she said. "It has nothing to do with who I am now."

Meldrum took a breath. "You say your husband left you for another woman?"

"Mmm. My sister."

"No." He pulled himself together. "I'm talking about Michael Thorne."

She nodded brightly. "Oh, yes. He did too." She laughed. "Not with my sister, I don't mean that."

"Could you tell me her name?"

"Whose name?"

"This woman your husband, Michael Thorne," he ignored her smile, "went off with."

"Why?"

"We have to know as much about him as we can. It's our best hoped of finding who killed him."

"Isn't that old fashioned?"

"Sorry?"

"Don't you have DNA for that nowadays?"

"Everything helps."

"Enemies," she said.

He made a guess. "You mean we're looking for enemies?"

"Someone who might have wanted to kill him." She smiled. "What about me? Would the deserted wife not be the one who had a grudge?"

"Had you?" McGuigan asked.

She let a moment pass. To Meldrum's surprise, the sergeant flushed as she eyed him with unhidden appreciation.

At last, she said, "If I'd been going to kill Michael, I'd have done it twenty years ago."

"How did your son feel about him?" McGuigan asked.

"What do you mean?"

She had stopped smiling.

"I'm wondering," McGuigan said, "why he calls himself Halliday instead of Thorne."

"Oh, really." She shook her head impatiently. "Colin was twenty-three when Halliday took himself off. He'd changed his name once. Why would he change it back again?"

Because he was upset that his stepfather had gone off with his aunt? Meldrum thought. He said nothing, though. He'd learned that it paid to give McGuigan his head.

"And because he was still angry with his real father?" McGuigan wondered.

"For God's sake, I didn't change back. Why on earth would he? He'd started work. Why embarrass himself? He left his name as it was, because it wasn't worth the bother." She got her smile back. "I know that's how I felt."

When McGuigan didn't respond, Meldrum decided to take up the questioning. He asked, "What was the name of that woman again? You didn't say."

She blinked at him. "The woman Michael went off with?"

"That's the one."

She tapped her fingers together, bending her head in what seemed to be a genuine effort to remember. "Isn't that silly? It can't have gone out of my head. Her name?" She rested her lips on the tips of her fingers. "Something common and vulgar. Might be acceptable enough nowadays, of course. It used to seem like that, though. Kind of name my grandmother would have given a housemaid. Bridget? Yes, Bridget! That was her name."

As they went down the stair, McGuigan said without emphasis, "Bridget."

Does he think I don't remember? Meldrum wondered. Think I'm losing my grip? It was possible he was losing his grip.

"The woman Michael Thorne still thought about — at least if the neighbour got it right." He tried but couldn't remember the name of the elderly neighbour who had told Thorne about his dead wife and had been laughed at for his pains.

"Calum Grant," McGuigan said in the same neutral tone.

CHAPTER
TWELVE

As Meldrum sipped his whisky, he looked up at the flow of images on the television fixed in the corner of the ceiling. Out of habit, he checked out three men talking, heads close together, at the bar. When McGuigan had asked, "Where to now?" he'd told him *nowhere*. In return he'd received a look of disbelief. At this stage of a murder enquiry, detectives didn't keep shop hours. We could go and try Colin Halliday, McGuigan had suggested, if he lives as close as the mother said. Refused again, with even his offer of a lift turned down, he'd gone off scowling. Meldrum had stood in the street outside the close until the car was out of sight, then slanted across the street to find a drink. He still had time to kill before he was due to meet his daughter.

As he drank, he went over again the interview with the mother. Was it possible she could be as indifferent to her first husband as she pretended? She hadn't shown any curiosity over the manner of Thorne's death. Certainly, no sign of being shocked. Even after a long separation, the violent death of someone you'd once been intimate with might have been expected to produce a response. Fleetingly, he thought of the second husband, Colin Halliday's stepfather, who'd eloped with his wife's sister. Mrs Halliday was a woman who seemed to have bad luck with men. Yet she'd given the impression of being ready, more than ready, to try again. Was that the defining characteristic of the unlucky ones?

And then there was Bridget ... Presumably the Bridget Michael Thorne had told that sad old neighbour of his he missed and thought of still. Thinking it over, it struck him that if she'd attracted Thorne from his wife something like twenty years ago, there was no reason why Bridget shouldn't still be alive. A man could mourn for a woman he'd lost without her being dead. Was she worth looking for? As he pondered, the beer came up sour on a belch into the back of his throat. He should get something to eat. Drinking in the late afternoon on an empty stomach was a bad idea.

His thoughts were interrupted by a shudder over his heart. He felt for the mobile and snapped it open.

"Hello?" A woman's voice, very soft, as if from somewhere far away.

"Betty?"

"I can't make it, Dad."

"Why not?"

"Just can't."

"You said you wanted to talk." He stared unseeingly at the television screen. The sound had been switched off and he watched the images move in silence. "Don't cut yourself off," he said. One of the men at the bar turned his head and Meldrum lowered his voice. "I hate for you to be so unhappy."

"Next week," she said. "We can meet next week."

"And you'll come? Don't do this to me again. I can't afford this. I have work to do." The moment the words were out of his mouth, he regretted them.

"I wouldn't want to keep you from your work." It might have been her mother speaking.

"Next week then," he said.

"Same place?"

"Sure. We'll find a quiet corner where we can talk. I'll phone at the weekend to confirm it."

"No!" she said. She went on more quietly, "Let me phone you. If you're not there, I'll keep trying till I get you. That would be the best idea."

"Is there a reason why I shouldn't phone you at Corrigan's?"

The man at the bar looked round again and said something at which the other two laughed.

"It's nothing to do with him. He took Tommy and me in. That's important, Dad. I mean we couldn't have come to you."

Meldrum sat silent. In his anger he wanted to say she didn't have to go to him or to her mother and Corrigan. She could have stayed on her own and still managed surely to care for the baby. But then he thought of the other baby who was dead and was ashamed.

"As long as everything's all right," he said quietly.

In her turn there was a long silence. At last, so faintly he strained to hear her, she said, "I'll phone."

There was the sound of the call being ended.

48

It was bad luck that the same man looked over his shoulder for the third time. When he saw Meldrum on his feet and moving towards him, he turned right round and hunched over his pint. A moment later, he sensed like a dark wind a presence at his back.

Looking down, Meldrum asked, "Do you want to share the joke?"

Two of them turned round and then stood. Both had to look up at him. The taller came almost to his shoulder.

One of them asked, "What the fuck's your problem?"

The hard man's response, but there wasn't any conviction in it.

Neither of them over twenty. Little fuckers, Meldrum thought. He wanted one of them to try something. The thing about little fuckers was one might be carrying a knife.

"We're not looking for trouble." It was the third one, the man hunched determinedly over his pint. He spoke without turning, staring down into the glass. When he looked over his shoulder, his face was slack with fright. "I think there's a misunderstanding." And then his eyes went shiny and he said, "I'm sorry."

Outside in the street, Meldrum found he was still clutching the mobile. He stuck it back in his inside pocket. When he took his hand out, he saw that it was trembling.

Christ, he thought. What's wrong with me?

CHAPTER
THIRTEEN

The assistant minister, whose name was Henry Porter, was tall and lean with close cut hair and an open friendly manner.

"My father," he volunteered as if either Meldrum or McGuigan looked likely to care, "was glad when I decided to come to Scotland. His grandmother came from Skye."

"Long way from here to Skye," McGuigan observed.

Porter laughed. "I come from Texas. Edinburgh to Skye would be nothing."

They were there to ask about the ministry of Michael Thorne, but the Revd Porter had the gift himself of extracting information and became intrigued by the question of Mrs Halliday's credentials as a Pentecostalist.

"Glossolalia is the dressed-in-its-Sunday-best name," he explained. "I wonder if this woman you mention was truly speaking in tongues. It doesn't mean babbling, you know, but using the languages of the world. I'll be frank with you, I can't recall anyone of that name being in attendance at church while I've been here."

"Maybe," McGuigan speculated, "she stopped coming after her husband left her."

"That should be when she most needed comforting."

"Might make it harder if your husband was the minister," McGuigan said.

"But he wasn't! At least not in this church. When you phoned, I accepted what you said. I've only been here three years so I didn't know, but when I asked I was assured Michael Thorne was never a minister here."

"Mrs Halliday told us he was," McGuigan said. Whether intentionally or not, it came easily to him to move into what sounded like threat mode.

Fearful perhaps for Mrs Halliday, Porter tried to make sense of it. "I have checked our records and with the dates you gave me, I found that a Michael Thorne and an Aileen Temple were married here."

As Meldrum glanced at McGuigan, he saw that the same thought had struck each of them. Mrs Halliday had spoken of having a vision of Jesus on the Musselburgh bus the day she was married. She had also spoken of speaking in tongues at a service conducted by Michael Thorne. They had taken it for granted that both events had been in Edinburgh. Even if Thorne had chosen to get married in Edinburgh, it now it seemed his ministry had been elsewhere.

"Is there any way," Meldrum asked, "that you could find where Thorne served as a minister?"

"The same thought occurred to me," Porter said, his eager goodwill undiminished. "I've haven't had much time since your call, I should say. But I did make some preliminary enquiries. OK, I was curious. It doesn't help that the Reverend Gillies is ill. I phoned around a few people but didn't have any luck. One of the congregation raised the possibility that even if he was a minister, it might not have been in Scotland."

It was a mess. The kind of mess policemen tried to avoid in front of civilians. As the two detectives sat in a scowling silence, the good-natured Porter administered an unwitting *coup de grace*.

"Wouldn't the simplest thing," he wondered, "be for you to go back and ask Mrs Halliday?"

CHAPTER
FOURTEEN

They spent the rest of the day backtracking on previous information, each time brought up short in one or another dead end. They couldn't find any friends and it could have been a rule of thumb that a man without friends likely as not didn't have enemies either. At one point, a frustrated McGuigan wondered whether it mattered if a blank slate like Michael Thorne was taken out of circulation. If it hadn't been for the awkward fact of the hole at the back of his skull, it would have been easy to believe no one cared whether he lived or died.

Having put off an interview neither was looking forward to, it was after five before they found themselves again at Mrs Halliday's door. They rang and repeated the process until it was obvious there would be no answer. Having checked beforehand on Colin Halliday's home address, there was no question as to where they would go next. Keeping a moody silence, they started up to the top of Marchmont Road.

This time the door opened almost before Meldrum took his hand from the bell.

"Thank God, you're back," the woman was saying as it opened.

Seeing the two men, her mouth hung on the last word before slowly closing.

Meldrum stared at her, matching her surprise. It hadn't occurred to him that Colin Halliday might have a partner.

"We're here to see Mr Halliday," he said.

"He's not here."

She stepped back. Before Meldrum could react, McGuigan had put his hand on the door. "You're expecting him back, though, aren't you?" he said.

His sergeant's gesture offended Meldrum. She'll think we're bloody moneylenders, he thought. His mind turned back to leaving his own flat the previous evening. Coming down the stairs, he'd heard a man's voice saying on a note of desperation, "We'll get it, we'll get it." He'd thought he recognised the voice. A couple had moved into the flat below his own and he'd marked them down at once as being on social security. Only the other morning he'd passed the woman dragging her small daughter with one hand while balancing bags and a go chair with the other, and shouting, "Shift yourself or I'll batter you, you stupid wee shite." She'd stepped back and bumped into him and offered in an entirely different tone, polite and apologetic, "Oh, here, I'm awful sorry." As he rounded the turn of the stair, he saw the door of the flat was open. In the doorway stood the woman with a child at her knees and her partner by her side but leaning out from the waist so that though his upper body was through the entrance the rest was trying to hide inside. The oddness of the body language struck Meldrum. It was as though the man wanted to

54

protect his woman and his child, but fear had rooted his feet to the spot. Confronting the two of them was an undersized runt of a man holding on a leash the biggest dog Meldrum had ever seen. Like a bloody Shetland pony, he'd thought. As he came in sight, the man glanced up at him. In a voice so softly reasonable that Meldrum hardly made out the words, he said, "Next week then," and went back the way he'd come, the dog's swaying haunches seeming to brush the landing wall on one side and the railing on the other. Bloody moneylenders, Meldrum had thought.

Even as the incident passed through his mind, he was trying to placate the woman in Halliday's flat by explaining who they were. "We really need a word with him. Do you know when he'll be back?"

She shook her head. He couldn't help noticing that despite her pallor, she was a good-looking woman. Perhaps in her mid-thirties, she had black hair to her shoulders, wide blue eyes, a strong nose and high cheekbones.

"Tell him to give me a call. Detective Inspector Meldrum. That's my number."

"What's it about?" At his look of inquiry, she hurried on, "I could tell him when he comes in."

"He'll know," Meldrum said.

She took the card and stepped back warily, as if waiting for him to push his way in before she could get the door closed.

"There's a surprise, eh?" McGuigan said as they started down. "I'd that arse down as a poof."

Before Meldrum could respond, Colin Halliday came stepping lightly round the bend of the stair towards them.

"What do you want?" he cried in a shrill voice.

Meldrum was startled by his look of fright.

"There was just a couple of things, sir."

Looking up at them, voice under control, he said, "Ask away then."

The detectives' response was to take a couple of steps backwards on to the landing. They moved in unison as if by an unspoken agreement.

"This isn't a suitable place, sir. Can we go inside?"

Halliday squeezed past them, fumbling his keys out of his coat pocket.

When they followed him into the hall, a long narrow straight passage with doors on either side, there was no sign of the woman.

"If we go along here," he said loudly as if projecting from a stage, "we can talk."

He led the way to the end of the passage where it turned a corner into a small square space with two doors. The one on the right lay half open to show a toilet. He opened the other and they followed him through into a big kitchen with a work surface littered with pot noodles and wrappers and carry out boxes. A pine table set round with upright chairs took up the middle of the floor. Halliday took off his coat, threw it over the back of one of the chairs and asked, "Well?"

"We went to see your mother, Mr Halliday."

"It's a long time since she was married to my father. I can't see how she would be much help to you."

"Thing is, she gave us the impression your father, Michael Thorne, was a Pentecostal minister —"

"He was."

"Here in Edinburgh?" Meldrum finished.

"No. Not here. I'm sure my mother never said that."

"Our mistake then. But the minister we spoke to tells us he checked the church record and found someone called Michael Thorne who married a woman called Aileen Temple thirty years ago. Can you confirm that would be your mother?"

"Her maiden name was Temple. They came to Edinburgh to get married. I don't know why. Maybe he had relatives here."

As Halliday answered, Meldrum watched the kitchen door behind him ease shut, just the tiniest of movements but enough to show it had been cracked a fraction open. Someone had been listening to them.

"And then what? Went back to his ministry? Back to his parish? Do you know where that would be?" Did they call it a parish?

"I suppose so. I wasn't born at that point."

Showing them out, Colin Halliday came to an abrupt halt at the beginning of the long passage. The woman who'd let them in earlier was standing half way along it. She didn't speak or move, just stood there until at last he muttered, "This is one of my flatmates," and went to squeeze past her.

"You found him," the woman said to Meldrum.

"We met Mr Halliday on the stairs."

"They wanted to ask about your father," she told Halliday.

"I'll tell you later." And looking back at Meldrum he explained again, "This is my flatmate. Shona Flett."

In the car, McGuigan said, "We didn't say anything to the woman about wanting to ask about his father."

"No."

After a moment, McGuigan said, "She was listening?"

"Other side of the door."

"Pretty nosey for a flatmate."

"Some folk are like that."

"But he said, I'll tell you about it. Do you think he's screwing her?"

"Maybe."

Coming up fast at Melville Drive behind an SUV as the lights changed, McGuigan had to brake a shade too hard. Normally an immaculate driver, he made a little exasperated noise. As they started moving again, he said, "Aye, maybe. She's a lot of woman. There's something about him though . . ." He trailed off. "Another thing. What did you make of the stuff in the kitchen?"

"The fast food lying about? It was a lot for two."

"Either that or they just let it pile up."

They drove on in silence.

CHAPTER
FIFTEEN

Bryd had lain awake during the night. That happened to her when she knew the Convenor would be with them on the following day. She would lie awake and know from the stirrings and soft sighs from the other beds that her companions were also passing a sleepless night. This last night, however, had been different. Her excitement and expectation had been complicated by the anxiety of what she had learned the previous day, and the overwhelming problem whether she should or could keep it to herself.

Sleepless, like a child afraid of the dark, she had lain with her eyes closed. When she opened them, her first reaction was bewilderment. It was Cadoc's job in the morning to waken all three women and make sure they rose at once. Yet Grania's bed under the window was empty, and the tall Emer was already standing between Bryd's and her own narrow bed. Emer's long red hair was loose around her shoulders and her head was bowed as if she had been stopped by some thought in the process of getting dressed. She had pulled on her pants, white lace ribboned in lilac; her legs rose on and on to the curve of her buttocks; clothed her breasts drew attention, naked they were spectacular, long, full and heavy, small nipples lightly circled, too firm to need support. Keeping very still, Bryd studied her through half closed eyes and thought, she's only nineteen.

Emer said softly, not raising her head, "He didn't waken us."

Bryd opened her eyes wide. She made a show of yawning and then swung her legs out of bed. As she dressed, she was conscious of the care she was taking not to look at Emer's body. Living together, sleeping in one room, normally they were unselfconscious, even with Cadoc. At the thought of him, she said, "No, he didn't."

"Could anything be wrong?"

"Get dressed and we'll go and see." And then at the girl's look of apprehension, she said quickly, "Of course, nothing's wrong. He and Grania will be sitting together having breakfast." Even as she spoke, she wondered if Cadoc had broken the routine because of what had happened the day before.

When they went into the kitchen, the other two were eating at the long table. The smell of coffee hung in the air and the kettle was boiling to refill the cafetiére. Cadoc loved coffee and said it was what kept him going.

Bryd waited for Emer to ask why they hadn't been wakened, but the girl took her place at the table without a word. Lost in her own thoughts, Bryd sat down, cut a slice from the loaf and laid strips of cheddar on it.

It was Cadoc who broke the silence.

"We went over budget this week. He won't be pleased."

It was part of their discipline to live as frugally as possible. Bryd picked up the teapot and felt by its weight that it was almost full.

Grania said, "I just made a new pot."

As Bryd poured, she said, "We have to eat, Colin."

She stopped abruptly, appalled at what she had said. Although they knew one another's names and used them when they were alone together, the Convenor insisted they address one another only by the names he had given them. It was a matter of security, they had been told. If I can't give your real name even under torture he told them, it may save your life. For this reason, there was a strict rule that they used only the names they had been given on any day when the Convenor was due to visit. That way there was less chance of blurting out a name; blurting it out as she had just done. Everything is changing, she thought. After the killing of the old man how can anything be the same?

The thought came back to her when they began to squabble. They had spent two hours making the flat perfect. The beds were made as if for a military inspection. Every surface was cleared and wiped and tidied. The furniture was polished, the floor hoovered. As they had learned to do, they worked as a team. Yet Bryd felt the new currents of something like fear, something like anger, something like dismay. The storm broke as the sound of church bells began, and it was she who triggered it.

Because the day before dominated her thoughts, she said, "If only we'd done all this yesterday."

"Why?" Grania asked sharply.

They were in the living room, everything almost finished, Cadoc and Grania already sitting side by side on the sofa, Emer and her putting the last touches to the room, more out of nerves than because anything was left to do.

She stood with the cloth in her hand, staring blankly at Grania, who asked again, "Why? What difference would it have made?"

She could not stop herself from glancing at Cadoc, but he gave nothing away and she realised that he had no intention of telling the others about the two policemen. How could she have imagined he would? What could he say to explain why they had come?

And suddenly Grania was in full flow. Trembling with rage, she said, "It's all right for you. Last night I was tired when I got back." She pointed at Emer. "So were you! Weren't you?" And when the younger girl said nothing her anger was deflected on to her. "Frightened to say? Don't be so bloody hopeless!"

"That's enough," Cadoc said.

It took you long enough, Bryd thought.

Too long. Grania started to shout at him, and then his voice was raised. Next moment, Emer was in tears and choking out some kind of protest. At last, Bryd found herself joining in and for a moment there was the release of four voices matching incoherence and anger that turned this way and that like a hose spraying acid.

The noise was at its peak when Bryd saw the Convenor standing watching. Within seconds, all of them had fallen silent. The only noise was the little sobs of Emer fighting to take breath. After a moment, he turned and they heard his footsteps going along towards the kitchen.

The room held its breath till he came back. They didn't look at one another as they waited.

When he came in, he was holding a container, which they recognised. Prising off the lid, he poured Cadoc's precious coffee out on to the carpet.

"After you get this cleaned up," he said, "we'll get down to why I'm here."

He held up an envelope. Bryd saw the stamp and knew it had come from Rome. The letter he drew from it was on heavy creamy paper with a seal at the top.

"It'll make you understand the danger we're all in and how many people are depending on us," he said.

CHAPTER
SIXTEEN

Betty phoned him before a week had passed.

"I can meet you tonight . . . if that's all right?"

It wasn't, but he told his daughter he would be there and lied and cancelled and let people down so that he might make it.

They met at just after nine, which was the earliest he could manage. It was a pub off the beaten track, down a flight of steps in a side street on the edge of the New Town. There were two couples already there, heads together, in opposite corners, as far away from one another as they could get, and so also, it seemed, wanting privacy. He sat her at a table and went to get drinks.

"Nothing's wrong?"

She made the face he had come to dislike, her mouth pursed up in a look of misery and self-pity. There was anger there, too, but then that had been true for a long time. Anger at the world, anger with him and his habit of asking stupid questions. Of course, nothing's wrong, her look said, everything's wrong.

He sipped at his pint and waited. He'd conducted a lot of interviews in the last twenty years. Waiting was a good idea. He knew things like that. It was unfortunate that, like many policemen's children, from being cross-questioned as a child she'd learned them too.

He broke first, but then he cared for her more than anyone in the world except her mother.

"Corrigan's not bothering you?"

"Why would you ask me that?"

He hadn't an answer to give her. In the course of an investigation, Meldrum had come across evidence that the man who'd married his ex-wife was the client of a prostitute who offered services out of the ordinary even in her line of work. He'd never told Carole or anyone else. He would have thought it just as wrong to tell Betty. But it didn't prevent him from distrusting and despising the man.

After a while, she said, "I know you don't like him. *I* hated it when Mum got married again. But he's been good to us. Tommy adores him."

"He tells a good story," Meldrum said.

"I hate that," she said.

"What?"

"When you make that face."

Carefully for a while they talked of more neutral matters, passing time with the things Tommy said that had made her smile and whether Carole was looking after herself properly.

"And you?" he asked. "How are you feeling?"

She frowned at him. "Are you asking when I'm going back to work?"

"If I want to know that, I'll ask you."

"Feeling?" She looked away from him, glancing down to the side. "Put it this way: I'm still taking the tablets."

She and her husband Sandy had met as student activists, the politics for him being more about her than any deep convictions. He had been studying art, and was one of the select few, not many in any year, who had some prospect of making it as a painter. Betty getting pregnant had meant that, instead of taking up a travelling scholarship, he'd taken a job as a teacher. Their love had survived that sacrifice. For a time, in the wreckage of his own life, Meldrum had taken pleasure in the father and mother and baby Sandy as the perfect family. Then the baby died. A childish ailment badly treated. Sitting in a hospital waiting room. Told there was nothing to worry about. Told the child was dead. Afterwards Betty had had a breakdown.

"I'll never forgive him," he said, and cursed himself for a fool as soon as the words were out of his mouth.

"You've no right to say that."

"If he loved you . . ." He didn't have to finish. If he loved you, he wouldn't have left you. "I'll never understand it."

"Maybe he'll get to be a painter again," she said. "Underneath everything else, he was unhappy about that all the time."

"So he should have painted. You weren't stopping him."

"You don't understand."

"A real man doesn't —"

"A real man." She mocked him.

Doesn't let anything stop him. Does what he has to do. Doesn't find excuses. What point was there in saying any of that?

66

"I thought better of him." Truth was, he had always admired his son-in-law. He struggled to find the right words. In a kind of apology, he said, "The death of wee Sandy altered everything. I know couples never get over the death of a child. So many of them break up."

"Can we leave this?"

"I never lost a child," he said and, looking at her, wondered if that was true. He knew that it would be a mistake to say any more. "All the same," he burst out, "you had another baby. How the hell could he walk away and leave his own son?"

"Christ," she said, "have you not worked it out? You're the only one that hasn't. Sandy isn't the father."

And the world didn't end. They talked, but not about what had been said. When enough time had passed, they went out and he saw her to her bus stop and they said goodbye. Neither mentioned meeting the next week, but that didn't mean that they wouldn't. It was possible that they would. He waved to her as the bus pulled away and her face looked out at him, white behind the smeared glass, and then he went and got drunk, which was no solution but a habit into which he'd fallen.

Hours later he finished up in the lounge of a hotel. He hadn't picked it deliberately, but it wasn't quite by chance. When he saw the prostitute at a table, there was a man with her, middle-aged and flush with drink, but not so flushed that he didn't squirm out of his seat and edge away when Meldrum leaned over them.

"What's your name again? Myra, was it? Not Mary. Come on, come on. Myra, was it?"

"You'd better sit down before you fall down," the woman said.

CHAPTER
SEVENTEEN

It was unreasonable to be irritated. When had a detective's load ever been fair? All the same, as they ran through Gullane, it seemed to him he had enough on his plate with the Michael Thorne enquiry; the bank clerk's rape nearing the cold case stage, a back file of serious assaults. Ten years ago, five even, he would have taken anything extra in his stride. Now the thought of another killing filled him with weariness. And McGuigan was driving again. When did that start to happen, he wondered, there had been a time when he did all the driving himself. He couldn't place when he had started being a passenger.

He felt McGuigan cut a glance across.

"Rough night?" the sergeant asked.

"No."

Second time he'd wakened in the prostitute's bed: Marie. Forget her name, he told himself. There wouldn't be a third time.

"Can't be far now," McGuigan said.

Shortly afterwards, they turned left and ran up into Dirleton, the ruined castle on their right, the village square and solid bulk of the kirk on their left.

"Everybody still asleep," McGuigan said.

Meldrum grunted. There was silence as they wound across the flat farmland towards the shore and came out on the open space of car parking. Police vehicles lined up at the far end in front of the tourist noticeboard. They started down in the direction of the beach, taking care to walk on the hard ground on either side of the sandy path. As they came out on to the open expanse of grassland, the grey mist creeping about the dunes was stirred by a soft wind. They picked their way across the tough marram grass to where officers were working around a temporary shelter. As they approached it, a heavy-footed crow, as if drawn to prey, refused to move and kept tugging at the body of a rabbit in the grass, one bright eye turned back on them as if miming indifference. Despite the hour, Meldrum wasn't surprised to see men, one alone, the other with a dog at his side, watching from a safe distance.

Together they ducked under the fluttering scene of crime ribbons.

"You senior here?" Meldrum asked a uniformed sergeant. "Get somebody over to talk to those two." He nodded towards the spectators.

"I didn't notice the guy with the dog," the sergeant said. "The other one found her. Says he's a photographer, he's got the gear. Says he came down to get birds at sunrise, you know the kind of stuff."

"Take him up and put him in a car. Find out who the creep with the dog is. And why the fuck is that path not sealed off?" The murderer and his victim had probably left the car park that way.

70

As men started bustling around, he followed McGuigan to the shelter.

Dr Fleming looked up from beside the corpse. "Never heard you swear before," he said interestedly.

The body lay face down. The back was white and unblemished. The waist neat. The buttocks round and full. Long black hair. One hand stretched out as if pointing. No injuries visible. No doubt that it was the body of a mature woman.

"Got anything?"

"I was just going to turn her over."

"Hold it for a minute." He stepped back and spoke to the sergeant. "Get it taped from the end of the path to here. Ten feet wide should do it." No sign of clothing which suggested she'd been killed somewhere else. If the murderer had carried her here, he wouldn't have done much wandering about. She didn't look like a lightweight.

He looked round in time to see Fleming turn the corpse.

"Christ!" somebody said.

Another voice muttered, "Some fucking madman."

The body had been mutilated. Red gouges marked both breasts and between the legs. At the unexpectedness of the sight, he surrendered to the image of the crow slashing its beak into the bloodied meat between her thighs and tasted sickness as a wave of nausea moved through him.

McGuigan said quietly, "We know her."

Meldrum lifted his eyes to the dead woman's face. It took a moment to place her. Agony made some kind of disguise.

"At Halliday's place," he said softly.

Fleming was looking up at them in curiosity.

"Yes," McGuigan said.

The name of the woman Colin Halliday had introduced them to came effortlessly to mind. Shona Flett. The violated woman had been called Shona Flett. Poor Shona Flett. Meldrum walked away. He kicked at the crow and put it to flight, passed the photographer being escorted back by a young constable and kept going until he came down from the dunes on to the beach.

He ploughed across the sand until he came to the edge of the water. The tide had turned and long waves were tumbling into the land. Like a rag hung out to dry, a black shag stood on a rock with its elbows raised.

He heard the smack of shoes slapping on the wet sand but didn't look round.

Behind him, McGuigan said, "Are you all right?"

"Rough night," Meldrum said.

The firth spread out before him, the sun turning the grey waters blue, the hills of Fife on the far side, the islands of Fidra and Lamb afloat on the last of the morning haar.

"We'd better get back."

They made their way across the sand, each busy with his own thoughts. They had climbed back on to the dunes and were almost back at the group around the body before the silence was broken.

"Did Colin Halliday look like a madman to you?" McGuigan asked.

CHAPTER
EIGHTEEN

They rang the bell and waited, then rang again. This time McGuigan didn't take his finger from the bellpush.

When Colin Halliday opened the door, his hair stood on end unbrushed and he clutched a dressing gown across his chest.

"What do you want?"

As Meldrum answered, he was walking forward, forcing Halliday to retreat into the hall. McGuigan closed the door behind him as he entered last.

"Have you been out of the house tonight?" Meldrum asked.

"What is this?" He opened the nearest door and looked inside. As he did they heard the chiming of a clock from the room. "Good God, it's only seven o'clock. What are you doing here? You've no right. I'll call the —" If he'd been going to say "police", the absurdity of that must have struck him, for he took a breath and used both hands to smooth down his hair. Pulling the cord of the gown tightly around his waist, he asked in a reasonably steady voice, "Do you have a warrant that lets you burst in here? This isn't Nazi Germany."

"Burst in?" Meldrum asked. He glanced at McGuigan. "Did we burst in?" Getting no answer, he went on, "When we told you why we were here, you invited us in. Be bloody odd, if you hadn't . . . under the circumstances."

Halliday started to speak, stopped and cleared his throat; tried again.

"Under what circumstances? Why *are* you here?"

"When did you last see Shona Flett?" Meldrum asked abruptly.

Two possibilities, he thought, looking at the expression on Halliday's face: either he's genuinely astonished or he's a wonderful actor.

"*Shona?* . . . Has something happened to her?"

"Could we . . .?" Meldrum gestured towards the door that had been opened.

Halliday went into the front room. Following, Meldrum took in an impression of a large room almost empty of furniture apart from an old couch and a couple of armchairs. There were no pictures on the walls, no television in sight. There was a fine marble mantlepiece, but the grate underneath was filled with crumpled newspapers. There didn't seem to be any heating. Despite the brightness outside, the chill in the air suggested a north facing room that didn't get any sunshine. Without being asked, he sat in one of the chairs, the leather cold against his back. After a moment's hesitation, McGuigan took the other chair. Reluctantly, Halliday subsided into the middle of the couch.

"Has Shona had an accident?" he asked. "She went to work yesterday morning. Didn't come back last night. I've been worrying about her."

"She was found dead just after dawn this morning," Meldrum said. He stood up. "The sergeant here will tell you about it. I need to pee."

Before either of them could say anything, he went out and shut the door behind him. He went quickly along the hall, opening doors as he went. The largest room he found had only one bed in it, a bed so narrow it could take only one sleeper. He opened a door to show a cupboard with a rail holding shirts and two suits. On the floor, there was a pile of shoes, which he sifted through quickly. Before he left, he crouched down and examined the carpet. In the light slanting from the windows, he made out deep indentations laid in patterns that suggested other beds had once been there. The room next door was only half the size and again held a single bed. There were women's clothes in a cupboard, and a chest of drawers with blouses and underwear. In the third room, he stood in the doorway looking at the dismantled carcasses of two beds stacked against a wall. At the end of the passage, he found the bathroom and, leaving the door open, flushed the toilet.

As he went back into the living room, McGuigan regarded him with a studied lack of expression. Halliday was bent forward, elbows on knees, holding his face between his hands. Lifting only his eyes, he said, "I can't believe it. What would she be doing out there? I don't understand."

"She was taken."

"Taken?"

"Chances are she was already dead. She could have been killed here."

"*Here?*"

"In town, I mean."

Halliday sat up. "She didn't come home last night."

"So you said. Can I ask what your relationship was with her?"

"Relationship?"

"You were living together."

"Not like that. Not the way you're suggesting."

"You were flatmates. I think that's what you said when you introduced her to us."

He shook his head. "That's not quite right. If I said she was my flatmate, I don't know why. Maybe I was embarrassed to say she was my landlady. Anyway, how was I to know it would ever be your business?"

"She owned the flat?" Meldrum was surprised. For no better reason, perhaps, than that "flatmates" had suggested to him that they were both tenants there. "Who else was living here?"

"No one."

"It's a large flat. I'd have thought if she was going to rent, she'd have wanted more than one boarder."

"You'd have to ask her!" Halliday said sharply, then winced. "I can't believe she's dead." For some reason, perhaps because someone who keeps silence draws attention, he looked to McGuigan. "I think she was hoping to get another boarder. Only thing is, she'd have had to do the place up first. It's pretty run down. Maybe that's what was stopping her."

76

McGuigan didn't respond.

"So there's no one to confirm she didn't come home last night?" Meldrum asked.

"I can confirm it," Halliday said firmly.

Meldrum grunted. "But she went off to work at her usual time?"

"Yes."

"Did she behave normally?"

"Yes!" He frowned. "As far as I noticed. It was the morning. We were both going to work. We were in a hurry. No need to talk. We made breakfast and went to work. Same as any other morning."

"Where did she work?"

"In a dress shop somewhere."

"You don't know where?"

"Sorry."

"Not even a rough idea?"

"She left about half eight. Caught a bus into town. Can't be more help than that. Sorry."

"What else can you tell me about her? Did she talk about her family?"

"Not to me."

"Friends?"

"No."

"How long have you been lodging here?"

"Must be almost three years." He pulled a face. "We didn't have a lot in common. Don't misunderstand me. We got on well enough. We just didn't sit around chatting."

"So there wasn't any kind of attraction between you?"

"No, there was not. It's very old-fashioned of you to think there might be. A man and woman can live in the same flat without — that kind of stuff. It happens all the time. In dozens of flats in this district. Don't you know that?"

As he had recovered his poise, his tone had become increasingly acerbic.

"I'm sure that's true," Meldrum said. "Can I ask, do you have a girlfriend?"

"You may ask, but you won't get an answer. It's none of your business."

Shortly afterwards, the two detectives emerged on to the landing. Instead of going down, Meldrum climbed to the top landing and began to knock each door on the way down. They had got back down into the close before his knock got a response. Told it was a police enquiry, the elderly man in carpet slippers, glasses on nose, still holding his paper, was eager to cooperate.

"There were four of them up there. The young fellow and three women. One of them was a real knockout. But I couldn't say I ever spoke to any of them. It's what they call multiple occupation. It's ruining Edinburgh. Students and DSS lets. Without good neighbours how can you get a close washed regularly or get roof repairs, eh? See across the road there? Have a look when you go out of the close. Dirty curtains hanging half off the rail. Another multiple occupation. Tinks and vagabonds. God knows what's going on in this city. Like everywhere else, it's going to hell."

A grim-faced McGuigan followed Meldrum back up the stairs.

When taxed with what they'd just been told, however, Halliday was unruffled.

"I didn't tell you she didn't have friends or have them visit her. I just said she didn't talk about them to me. And they certainly didn't live here."

CHAPTER
NINETEEN

Too busy with his own thoughts to pay attention to McGuigan being stone-faced and withdrawn as he drove them to see Shona Flett's parents, the outburst was finally provoked by Meldrum going over things aloud in an effort to organise his thoughts.

"I'm inclined to believe the neighbour," he said, gazing out unseeingly at the crowded morning pavements of Morningside. "All right, he was on the bottom floor so he didn't actually see them going into the flat. But he saw them going back and forward and swears there wasn't just Halliday and Shona Flett but two other women as well. That fits with the beds."

"Beds?" McGuigan let the syllable escape through tight lips.

"There's one big room with just the one bed in it. Halliday's, since he's got clothes and shoes in a cupboard beside it. Incidentally, I looked through the shoes. No sign of sand on any of them. There's a smaller bedroom with a single bed and there's women's stuff in there. Assume that was used by Shona Flett. But then there's another room with two dismantled beds in it. And the big room, Halliday's, for the sake of argument, has the marks of other beds on the carpet. It makes no sense, but I think there were four of them and all sleeping in the one room."

"Shoes," McGuigan hissed softly in rage. "Have you lost it altogether?"

"What?" Meldrum swung round startled.

"You pushed your way in, he didn't ask us. Then you go off and conduct a search? What would have happened if he'd come out and caught you? We didn't have a search warrant. We don't even have reasonable suspicion. We'd have been in a hell of a lot of trouble." He paused. "No. You'd have been in trouble. As far as I was concerned, you were taking a leak."

"You finished?" Meldrum asked softly.

"I don't know what's wrong with you."

"Don't worry about it."

"It's as if you don't care any more." He hesitated and then, the dam being broken, couldn't stop himself. "Long as you understand, you're on your own. No way I'm going down the tubes with you."

"Aye," Meldrum drawled. "You're an ambitious lad. What makes you think getting on the wrong side of me's a good idea?"

They drove the rest of the way, up Colinton Road and past the Braid Hills park entrance to the big houses on the crest of the hill, in silence.

CHAPTER
TWENTY

Alistair Flett was in his fifties, a corpulent man with a soft mouth and several chins. He plodded ahead of them through the house and out into a conservatory large enough to hold a dining table at one end and seven or eight cane chairs at the other. The light of the sun playing on the glass produced a hard whiteness that hammered nails into Meldrum's eyes. Flett sank into one of the chairs. After a moment, as he looked up at them in silence, his chin began to quiver, slightly at first and then worsening until his whole face trembled.

"You don't have to tell me," he said. "A journalist was here."

"That shouldn't have happened," Meldrum said. "If you give me his name —"

"It's true then?"

"You've been told that your daughter is dead?"

"I've been told she was murdered. I've been told she was naked. Where was it?"

"Her body was found on the shore at Yellowcraigs. That's not far from North Berwick."

"That journalist told me. But the name went out of my head. Yellowcraigs." He nodded his head slowly. "There's a car park, isn't that right? My wife and I would leave the car. Walk into North Berwick for lunch. Along the beach. That was when we lived in Longniddry. When we weren't long married. Before Shona was born." Each short sentence ended on a slight gasp as if his lungs had run out of air. "My wife won't be able to talk to you. She's upstairs in bed under sedation. The doctor's a family friend."

Outside the glass, Meldrum was conscious of how much lawn there was, how many flowerbeds, of the apple trees espaliered against a length of wall. Edinburgh was a small city, full of ample space concealed behind house fronts and garden walls.

"My main purpose in coming was to break the news to you myself," Meldrum said. "If you need time . . . I will have to talk to you but it doesn't have to be today."

"Ask me now. Otherwise I'll just be sitting." He shivered despite the stifling heat. "I came out here because I was cold."

"Could you tell me if your daughter was in a close relationship with anyone?"

Flett looked at him blankly.

"Mr Flett?"

"How would I know? I haven't spoken to her for years."

"Sorry? But you lived — she didn't live far away." From her flat to her parents' house had been no more than a fifteen minute car run.

"I know where she lived. I should, it belonged to my mother. Shall I tell you the truth? That was the cause of our quarrel. I've been sitting here thinking about it. When my mother died, she left everything, the flat, stocks and bonds, her jewellery, everything to Shona. I was upset since I'd counted on something. The business wasn't in trouble, but there was need for a cash injection. I explained that to Shona, but she wouldn't give up a penny, not even as a loan. Of course, I was angry. But I never meant it to go on and on. When she tried at first to make things better, I refused. And when I came to my senses, for some reason it was too late. She was cut off from us. Isn't that a terrible thing?"

What was there to say? It was a terrible thing. People with money valued it, sometimes too much. Neither there as minister or doctor, however, Meldrum stuck to his own task.

"Is there anyone we should speak to who might have been in touch with Shona?"

"She had one close friend. That was part of the trouble, I think. The two of them had plans." He trailed off and stared out at the sundrenched garden.

"Could you tell us how to contact him?"

His eyes focused again. "Him? I didn't say 'him', did I? Charlotte Tranter — they were at school together. She lived just along the road — her mother still does. It was easy for them to be friends."

"No one else you can think of?"

He shook his head.

"Would you ask your wife to think about it? If she can think of anyone?"

"She's sedated," Flett said. "How can I possibly ask her to — *Christ!* What planet are you people from?"

"I'll speak to her, when she feels better," Meldrum said. "I'm sure she'll want whoever did this to be caught."

"Feels better?" Flett said. "You'll have a long wait."

Yet, as he showed them to the door, he leaned close and said, "That journalist who came here — his name was Chris something-or-other — a tall thin streak of misery, stinking of cigarettes. What he did, coming here, he needs sorting out."

As he spoke, the planes of his face tightened into an image harder and more resolved, so that Meldrum could see the man who had quarrelled with his daughter because she refused to loan him money.

CHAPTER
TWENTY-ONE

"We spoke to your mother," Meldrum explained. "She told us you'd be in the shop."

"Boutique," Charlotte Tranter said. She was a tall thirty-something blonde with a ready smile that had switched off when she'd been told they were policemen. She stood, one hand resting on the back of a chair, poised to get them out of her life as quickly as possible.

The front of the shop, full of dresses on racks, blouses and matched accessories, made a contrast to this cramped back room with a table and four wooden seats round it, an electric kettle and a Baby Belling cooker with a bread board on top.

"I can't be away for too long," she said. "My assistants are good, but some customers prefer me to deal with them in person."

"We'll try to be quick."

"Something about Shona Flett? Sorry, I can't see how I could help. Has she got herself into trouble?" She gave a tight smile. "I doubt if she'd be turning to me for a character reference, if she has."

"I'm sorry to have to tell you Miss Flett is dead," Meldrum said.

Before he could go on, there was a light tap on the door and a young woman in a short, tight black dress put her head into the room. "Excuse me, Miss Tranter, but Mrs Crombie would like a word. She's quite insistent."

"Tell her I'll only be a moment." As the assistant left, Charlotte Tranter said, "I'm terribly shocked. I didn't even know she'd been ill."

"She wasn't," McGuigan said. For the sergeant's sake, Meldrum was relieved to hear him engaged again. "Her body was found near North Berwick early this morning. She'd been murdered."

Charlotte Tranter pulled the chair back, squeaking across the linoleum flooring, and sat down. Around the carefully applied make up, her skin showed in white patches.

"What an awful thing. North Berwick? Did she know anyone there? Who would want to harm her? What kind of people has she been mixing with?" She put a hand to her mouth. "I'm sorry, I can't get my head round it. We were at school together."

"Your mother said you were very close. Devoted friends, was the way she put it."

"We were. Did my mother say we were partners in this?" Her hand movement indicated the shop outside with its racks of dresses. "We both put money into it, but most of it was Shona's. Her grandmother had just died and she'd inherited and it was something we'd both talked about since we were girls. It was a dream come true. And then one day after we'd been open for three years, she told me she wanted to sell up. I was devastated."

"When was this?" McGuigan again, back in harness.

"It must be," her lips moved, "seven years ago. She wouldn't be moved. She wanted to realise her money. There was no reasoning with her. I had two choices — sell up or buy her out. I bought her out. It was hard —"

A tapping on the door was followed by the same assistant. As she took in Miss Tranter's distress, her eyes widened with the hint of scandal and she came in a little further before murmuring, "What should I say to Mrs Crombie?"

"Give her my apologies." And then as the assistant was turning away, "Wait! Tell her I've just been told of — of a death in the family."

After the girl had left on a flurry of gratified sympathy, Charlotte Tranter exclaimed, "There was a man! I'm talking about years ago. We'd started the business, and it was wonderful. Not that there weren't problems, but we always found a way round them. We just knew things were going to be a success. Every day was an adventure, that's the way it felt to me, to her too, I'm sure she felt the same. But then, she lost interest. I don't know how else to put it. It was as if she stopped being there, not physically, not at first, but as if she was always thinking of something else even when she was here."

"You think she was having a love affair?"

"A man would wait for her outside the shop. And then that stopped, but I was so worried, I followed her one night and he was waiting for her in the side street where she parked her car."

"The same man?"

"Oh, yes."

"Could you describe him?"

"It was such a long time ago."

"Anything at all. Height? Colouring? Age?" Meldrum asked.

"He was tall. I mean easily a head taller than Shona, and she was quite tall for a woman. Dark hair. I couldn't say about his age. He was a grown man, I mean he wasn't young."

Dark hair. Not Colin Halliday then, Meldrum thought.

"You think this man might have something to do with her wanting to sell her interest in your business?"

"I don't know. The whole thing was so inexplicable. She was so secretive about him. It was after I asked her about him that he stopped coming to collect her from the shop. I asked her mother about him, and that caused a row. Shona shouted at me — we hadn't ever quarrelled before that."

"It's our understanding that she'd fallen out with her parents."

"She wasn't living at home. But she still saw her mother — in secret, her father didn't know."

"Do you think she told her mother about this man?"

"I had the impression Mrs Flett wasn't surprised when I asked her about him. But that's all it was, just an impression. Anyway, whether she knew something or not, she wasn't sharing it with me. It was awkward for me going to her at all, even although she'd been like a second mother to me."

"Why would that be?" Habit made Meldrum work to the principle that once a witness started, the main thing was to keep them talking.

"Shona's father was angry with her because of the money she'd put into the boutique. I felt as if it was somehow my fault, although it wasn't. Obviously not."

"Did you ever see this man again?"

"No, not after Shona took herself off."

"Would you recognise him if you ever did see him again?"

She made as if to offer a quick response, then thought about it. "I'm not sure. I might pass him in the street and never notice. It's years ago . . ."

"But?"

"I never spoke to him. Never had more than a few glimpses. But there was something about him. That time I followed her and saw them together. She was looking up at him as if he — I can't describe it."

"As if she was . . ." He trailed off not wanting to influence her answer.

"Like something out of Mills and Boon, is what I thought at the time."

"As if she was in love with him?"

"More than that. Mills and Boon, you know."

Meldrum said, "I've never read Mills and Boon." A glance at McGuigan showed that the sergeant for once was equally at a loss.

"Oh, doctors and nurses, you know. Aristocrats and governesses. Tall dark strangers who are mysterious and a little bit frightening —" She broke off embarrassed. "How did I get into this? If you'd read them, you'd know what I mean."

Meldrum wondered if seeing the world that way helped her sell frocks.

He said, "You've been very helpful. We should let you get back to your customers."

"Clients," she said, getting up.

"Oh, one last thing."

"Yes?" Poised again for escape.

"Did you ever hear Miss Flett mention a man called Colin Halliday?"

"Never heard of him."

Outside, as they walked back to the car, McGuigan wondered, "What made you ask about Halliday? The mystery man's description didn't fit him. Oh, you were thinking his hair might be dyed? It looked natural to me."

"Maybe, when Charlotte Tranter saw him, it was dyed black," Meldrum said.

McGuigan was silenced, which was satisfying, even if neither of them believed it for a minute.

Anyway, asking hadn't been a waste of time.

"Never heard of him," Charlotte Tranter had said. "Can I ask who he is?"

"He'll probably get a mention in the papers. He was Miss Flett's lodger."

"Lodger? *Lodger?* Are you joking?"

"Of course not."

"Why on earth would Shona need a lodger?" Her tone held the word as if with tongs. "Apart from the flat, her grandmother left her half a million pounds."

CHAPTER
TWENTY-TWO

Meldrum knew the morning conference wasn't going well. Like a pack of hunting dogs, detectives responded to a scent, ran with it, the promise of a conclusion making up for the long hours and the spells of routine. Without it, they were slack, reluctant, going through the motions. It was also a matter of leadership, of course. If the pack leader had lost the place, the dogs circled, yawned and licked their balls.

"So are we any further forward with finding where Michael Thorne ate his dinner?"

Houston, who by coincidence Meldrum noticed was scratching his balls, shook his head. "Nothing so far, boss. We've just about run out of places to try."

MacIntosh, one of the others tasked with finding the dinner spot, pulled at his long nose, scratched his sandy mop of hair, and said in a throwaway tone, "Taken more time than you expected, boss? Is there something else we might be better doing?"

"If there was, I'd have said," Meldrum retorted, not entirely repressing a hint of a snarl. "If he follows the pattern, then he ate out at the same place every night. We need to know where that was. Maybe he met someone there. We haven't many other leads to follow.

We've spoken to the Pentecostal Church in England where he worked as a minister. It was a dead end. With a bit of persuasion, we got the contact to confirm that Thorne had served as a minister there, and that he'd gone off to Scotland to get married and had brought his wife back. And then the marriage broke up — and the two of them left — for Scotland presumably, the contact said." In a tone not much different from "for outer darkness." *Presumably*. Aye, right. "Mrs Halliday claimed that Thorne left her for a woman called Bridget. But the contact down there had never heard of Thorne in connection with a woman called Bridget."

"Would it not be worth having another go at Mrs Halliday?" Sharkey asked.

Since Sharkey was the third detective condemned to slogging around cafés and restaurants, Meldrum took this as another implied criticism. "Why didn't I think of that?" he asked sourly; and answered his own question, "Because according to her son, she's gone off on holiday. For a fortnight or so, the son thinks. To a flat her husband — the Halliday one — left her in Torremolinos."

There was what might at best be described as a thoughtful silence. Meldrum looked round the room at Edinburgh's finest studying their toecaps or eyeing the ceiling rather than meeting his eye. The silence was broken by Sharkey muttering to his neighbour.

"What?" Meldrum barked.

"Nothing." Then he grinned. "I was just saying I went on holiday to Torremolinos one time. There was a big slab up on the promenade and you could see the shit floating down the drain. I took a picture of it."

This was greeted by a mix of grunts of amusement and sighs that said, Fuck, it's only Tommy. Tommy Sharkey, Meldrum thought, the class clown.

"Which brings us," he said, as if Sharkey hadn't spoken at all, "to the two women one of Colin Halliday's neighbours claim were living in the flat as well as Shona Flett."

"Halliday and three women," MacIntosh said. "Was he having sex with one of them?"

"Or all of them?" Petrie said. There was a sense of him exerting himself. He and Lang were on the Flett murder team.

As if picking up on the tensions, McGuigan said, "It's hard to keep the two murders straight when the teams are mixed like this."

It annoyed Meldrum that the sergeant should give even the appearance of being at odds with him.

"They have a link," Meldrum said. "Halliday. First victim his father and the second the woman he lived with —"

"His landlady," McGuigan said.

"Still too much of a coincidence to ignore," Meldrum ploughed on.

"I just think we should keep an open mind," McGuigan persisted. "The cause of death is very different — stabbed in the skull for Thorne, strangled for Shona Flett. If a profiler was looking at them, I'd guess he'd come up with two different profiles." Meldrum wondered if McGuigan knew how sceptical he was of profilers. He couldn't remember if that had ever come up during the time they'd worked together. "And there is no robbery motive for Thorne — nothing much in the house, no will and nothing worth killing him for. But Shona Flett inherited half a million and a flat probably worth another three or four hundred — people have been killed for a lot less."

Meldrum could taste a faint unplaceable sourness lingering at the back of his mouth. Below his lower front teeth, his tongue rubbed slowly against a rough patch on his gum. He'd been in hospital once waiting for an operation after a stab wound, and the man he shared the ward with had shown him a patch of white roughness towards the back of his throat — they tell me I might lose my tongue, he'd said, and I've always loved amateur dramatics.

The room was silent. Meldrum became aware of the faces watching him. What the hell had they been talking about? It took an effort to remember. What would they say, he wondered, if I told them I've lost the place?

He said, "I've arranged to see Shona Flett's lawyer this afternoon. If Colin Halliday inherited her money," heads nodding around the room indicated the general belief that he had, "then we put everything into going after him."

CHAPTER
TWENTY-THREE

Grania shivered in the night. The flat in Marchmont had been without heating, but the four of them had slept in the same bedroom and, even in winter, some warmth had been generated from the flats above and below. Now she was in a room on her own, and this old house with its thick walls, half way up a hill and half way along a valley that curved up into still higher hills, had cold in its bones. To add to its discomforts, the month of September had begun with dark skies and a rawness of rain and wind from the northeast. When the first morning light came, she struggled with herself. The rule was to get out of bed as soon as wakening, or being wakened by Cadoc. Since it hadn't been part of the emergency that he should stay with them, she curled into a ball, trying to enclose whatever warmth she had generated, until the sound of a toilet being flushed brought her out of bed bare footed to be shocked into immobility by the cold striking up from the worn and faded linoleum.

She huddled into her clothes, piled unfolded on the chair where she'd dropped them, tights, bra, pants, a long skirt that came to her ankles and two jerseys one on top of the other. As she left the bedroom, Emer still in pyjamas was coming out of the bathroom.

"God," Grania exclaimed, "you'll get pneumonia."

"If you take a shower, be prepared. There's no hot water."

"How are we going to live here?"

"At least we'll live."

Squatting on the toilet, a morning ritual she normally enjoyed, had all the attraction of balancing on a column of ice. Finished, she washed her hands, rubbed them over her face and called that enough hygiene, more than enough. She found it hard to believe that Emer had been hardy enough to stand under a cold shower. It would be true, though. Emer told the truth. At nineteen, the girl was only five years younger than she was, but there was something about her, call it naïve, avoid the word innocent. Maybe it was because she was going to be a teacher in a primary school, her target audience seven-year-olds. That was nonsense, of course; there were girls doing the same course, heading for the same audience of tots, who were sexual predators; and lots of others who were tutor-smart, manipulating and conniving for grades. Grania, with a degree in maths under her belt and aiming for a target audience of seventeen year olds, had shared the campus with girls like Emer during her post-graduate year of teacher training. From that lofty height, she'd studied them as an anthropologist might notice the resemblances and radical differences between herself and a tribe of pygmies. And then in the third term of that short academic year, Cadoc had led her to the Convenor, and everything had changed. Shuddering with cold, she looked at her face in the smeared mirror above the wash basin and wept quietly in case she would be overheard.

After they'd eaten, they sat facing one another over the bare pine table. Through the window behind Emer, Grania could see a dry stone wall and sheep beyond it cropping a slope of rough grass. The silence went on unbroken until she couldn't bear it. "What are we going to do, Keeley?" she asked.

"Emer."

"We're alone!"

"All the same."

"Why?" When they were alone, it was Colin and Shona, Sandra and Keeley.

"We haven't a car," Emer said, as if that explained anything. Grania stared back at her in silence. She was wearing jeans and a light top. Doesn't she feel the cold? Grania wondered. She hadn't even the comfort of thinking it was an extra layer of fat that protected the younger woman, who was in fact tall and slim. Taller than her, slimmer than her. Younger, too, though not by much. And somehow not prone to feeling cold. "There isn't much food in the cupboard. I think the Convenor will come today. He won't leave us to starve. Let's be Grania and Emer today, in case he comes."

Grania frowned at her. "For God's sake! Who's talking about starving? Nobody's going to starve. We won't starve. There's a village we came through to get here. If we have to, we'll walk down and get food."

Emer stared in fright. "We were told to stay here," she said.

"I didn't say we *should* go down to the village. I just said that we could. If we were desperate. But if anybody comes today it will be Cadoc. After he finishes work."

"Why today? He didn't come back yesterday."

"We had enough food yesterday." Mention of work had changed Grania's thoughts into a different channel. "If we don't go into work . . ." School for her; college for Emer. "I can't just not go in."

"You could phone your school. Tell them you're sick."

"There isn't a phone in the house. I've looked."

"I thought there would be a phone."

"I can't see one."

Emer shrugged. "It could be on a shelf. Tucked away somewhere — I mean if the house hasn't been occupied for some time."

Grania jumped up. She went through the cold passage to the back door and went outside. Arms wrapped around her, she studied the outside of the house, came back in and took her place again at the table.

"No wires," she said, her teeth chattering.

"Eh?"

"This far out, there would be wires to bring a phone in."

They sat thinking about that until Emer said, "Use your mobile!"

"Cadoc took it."

"Why would he do that?"

Cadoc had shaken them awake at five in the morning, hours before their usual time. "Get dressed," he'd said. "We have to leave." Why? Why? *Why?* "Orders!" he'd said.

"What about yours?" Grania asked. "Did he take it as well?"

Emer went out. Her feet sounded on the uncarpeted stairs.

When she came back, she said, "I thought it was in my bag. It wasn't."

"Do you think he took it?"

At the question, Emer startled her by jumping up in the action of sitting. The chair tumbled over behind her with a crash.

"What does it matter?" she cried. "We were told to stay here. Let's do what we were told. There has to be a reason. Unless we know what it is, we don't know what to do. Can't you see you could ruin everything?"

Disoriented, Grania had no answer. She put her hands over her ears to shut out the shrill emphatic voice.

"Maybe the wires come in at the front," she said. "I should have looked."

It seemed even rawer when she went outside the second time. Again she'd gone out without putting on a coat. Wrapped in her arms as if holding herself together, she picked her way over the broken slabs at the side of the house. The hill opposite was marred on one slope by a scattering of burnt, black and twisted trees like a picture she had seen of a First World War battlefield. She crossed to the other side of the narrow road, unpaved, not much better than a track, to get a view of the house. Grey stone, mean windows to keep out the winter gale, a calor gas tank at the side, eight chimneys without smoke. There were no overhead wires.

As she studied the house, she heard the noise of a car coming up from the road below. It was hidden by a clump of bushes, but before she could move it swung into sight, a big car, taking the hill without effort.

She had time to think how it was too early to be Cadoc and that anyway it wasn't his car, when it turned into the yard, the door was wrenched open and the Convenor stepped out.

As she ran across the road, he shouted in a great bellow, veins standing out on his neck, "Get inside!"

In a panic, she fled past him to the front door, but it was locked. She turned the handle one way and the other, and then instead of knocking took to her heels round the side of the house. She caught her toe on one of the broken slabs and fell heavily. As she crouched sobbing for breath, a hand closed round her upper arm and lifted her to her feet.

To Emer, he came in like a storm carrying Grania in the swirl of his force. Her heart paused, breath choked in her throat. The two of them passed through into the hall. He didn't seem to notice she was there, but Grania cast one look, the whites of her eyes showing around the irises, pupils wide as if drugged. Alone she saw that she had thrown out her hands in appeal and slowly lowered them. She saw without moving, minutes passed as she waited. Her senses were unnaturally sharp, the drip from the tap rang like a beaten drum, but she heard nothing from the hall.

The door opened and as he came in the Convenor was folding a paper that he slid into the pocket of his coat. Reaching behind him, not needing to look, he took the pen Grania was holding out to him. Emer saw that she was weeping and trembling.

"Oh God," she said. "It's so awful."

"What is it?" Emer cried starting up in panic.

"Sit."

He stood looking down at them as they sat side by side. He looked from one to the other, holding each one's gaze until it seemed to the women that they would die if he did not speak.

When he did, his voice was so quiet that they had to strain to understand.

"I've done you a great wrong. God forgive me." They looked at him in terror. "Shona Flett is dead," he said, looking at Emer.

Stupidly, perhaps to hide the meaning of what he had said from herself, Emer cried, "Bryd!"

"Not Bryd any longer. No need to hide her real name from me. Not any longer." His voice trembled, which filled them with horror. "In the early hours of yesterday morning, my phone rang wakening me out of sleep. A voice told me that the woman I knew as Bryd was Shona Flett and that she had been killed. I won't describe to you the filth that voice poured into my ears about her nakedness and how she had been mutilated. I kept trying to tell myself it was a nightmare. After all the precautions we'd taken, it was impossible that they could have known who Bryd was. When I had taken it in, I cursed them, and told them to come and get *me* if they dared. 'Not yet', the voice said. I called Cadoc and instructed him to get you out of the flat. That's why you were brought to a place where you would be safe. To get here, I drove around back roads and doubled and checked and circled and I would swear to God I was not followed." He passed a hand over his face. "And all the time, I heard a voice telling me, 'Not yet'."

"But are we safe here?" Emer cried.

When the Convenor nodded slowly, Emer gave a sob of what must have been relief for she began to plead with him that they stay in hiding there. At this Grania found herself thinking, But we can't stay here. It seemed impossible to her. Perhaps the difference between us, Grania thought, is that she doesn't feel the cold. For herself, it seemed she might die of the cold. The idea of Bryd lying dead and naked somewhere — mutilated? what could that mean? — wasn't real, she refused to let it be real. The cold was real to her.

As if he could read her thoughts, the Convenor said, "If you want, I'll put you both in the car and take you to any city in the country. Maybe they won't find you."

"Don't leave us," Emer begged. "You have to look after us."

"You give me courage," he said.

He reached out and she got up and went to him and took his outstretched hand. As he led her from the room, he told Grania, "Stay here."

As she sat, her thoughts were inchoate, streaming, unformed, images and scenes passing like lit carriages thundering past a platform. An image of hunger and empty shelves brought her to her feet. She went out into the hall and looked in turn into each of the downstairs rooms. As she went silently up the stairs, her heart beat as if it would shake itself from her chest, and yet she told herself she was going to find them only in case he went off without being told that they had no food. All the same, she went straight to the bedroom door and listened. He had slept with Bryd, she had known that, but then he had known Bryd before any of them. Even so, once he had taken her also into his bed, she had been jealous of Bryd. The thought stabbed her now with shame. Emer, though, was a child. As she listened, she heard a shrill cry like a wounded creature and turned softly away. All thought of how they would survive driven from her head, she crept downstairs again as if the guilt were hers.

CHAPTER
TWENTY-FOUR

There had been a misunderstanding. The lawyer to whom Shona Flett's parents had referred Meldrum confirmed their opinion that she had never made a will. "Why on earth would she?" the elderly lawyer asked rhetorically. "A healthy young woman like that? Young people don't prepare themselves for dying in my experience."

All the same, further enquiry uncovered a will and the lawyer who had made it; a lawyer the Fletts had never heard of and yet not one, as it turned out, that Shona had found for herself.

Lester Peters was a different generation and a different stamp from the family lawyer who had philosophised for them on the heedlessness of the young. As it turned out, Meldrum had encountered him in the past acting in defence of one or another exponent of violent assault, drug dealer or money lender's enforcer. In his mid-thirties, he gave every sign of enjoying their mutual recognition.

Leaning back behind his desk, he confided, "I never much liked being a criminal lawyer. All right in Glasgow, maybe, no shortage of work there. I was glad to get out of it." He laughed. "Such a pleasure not to have to tell my clients to go away and come back when they'd found themselves a suit and a collar and tie."

"Can we talk about Shona Flett?"

"Terrible thing," his face composed itself instantly. "She sat in that chair you're in now." His eyes shifted to McGuigan. "And Mr Crowe in the one you're in. I can picture them now."

"Crowe?" Meldrum asked.

"Antony Crowe," the lawyer explained.

"Who's Antony Crowe?"

Peters exchanged the outward show of respect for the victim for what looked like a genuine puzzlement. "But I had the impression you had an idea who the heir might be."

"I'm not with you."

"Antony Crowe is the sole heir. Miss Flett left everything to him."

"Can you describe this man?" Meldrum asked.

"I think so. About six feet. Very black hair. Strong face, well marked eyebrows. Oh, and I remember thinking his nose had been broken at some time. Not the kind of chap you'd want to argue with. Blue suit, well cut, made to measure I should think."

Not Colin Halliday under another name, then. For some reason, he thought of the boutique owner Charlotte Tranter and the man she'd talked of who'd waited outside the shop.

"That's a good description," McGuigan said. "When was he here?"

"I can look up the diary for an exact date. Weeks not months."

107

Meldrum glanced at McGuigan, whose face showed no sign of what he was thinking. For himself, Meldrum was totally taken aback. Once he would have assumed that his own expression would have given no hint of that. Now, he was no longer sure. As if sensing a gap that needed to be filled, McGuigan asked, "What do you know about this Crowe? Was he a relative?"

"I shouldn't think so."

"Did the will give any reason why he had been made the heir?" Meldrum asked.

"None at all. The legalities, nothing personal. A perfectly sound will. Not one that would be set aside." He looked shrewdly from one to the other. "Unless for a very good cause."

"What do you have in mind?"

"Me? Nothing, nothing at all." Despite his profession, a man of no great discretion he couldn't resist adding, "Miss Flett was murdered, of course." And as the two detectives looked at him silently, he went on, "I suppose you might think it odd that it was Mr Crowe who first came to see me. He told me that he had a friend who wanted to draw up a will. I made an appointment and the two of them came in together the following day. It did seem . . . irregular."

"Who witnessed the will?"

"My secretary. The whole thing was done and witnessed in about twenty minutes. A flat in Marchmont and a bank account. Very straightforward, everything to him."

"That's an estate of almost a million pounds," McGuigan said.

"Oh, no. Nothing like. Not unless house prices are even madder than I think."

"The bank account?"

"Seventy thousand pounds. Nice to get, but not a big sum by today's standards."

In that case, Meldrum thought, what happened to the five hundred thousand her grandmother had left Shona Flett?

CHAPTER
TWENTY-FIVE

Shona Flett's mother had the blurred intent look of someone on heavy tranquillisers.

"We don't know anybody called Crowe." She turned to her husband for reassurance. "We don't, do we?"

Giving her a look of faint irritation, which was probably habitual, he didn't bother to answer.

"Did he know Shona?" he asked. "Is that why you're asking?"

"Yes," Meldrum admitted, "you could say he knew her."

"We haven't spoken to Shona in years," he said. "But we told you that." The soft plump-lipped mouth folded petulantly. "I don't see why you should come here thinking we'd know some acquaintance she's made."

"More than an acquaintance," McGuigan said.

"Please!" He held a hand up in protest. "Neither my wife nor I care about her private life. I'd be grateful if you kept the sordid details to yourself."

"I don't know about sordid," McGuigan said. "He's the one she left all her money to."

"What?"

Reading the word "liar!" in the flush of rage on Flett's cheeks, Meldrum intervened. "There was a will after all," he said quietly.

"There can't be!"

"We've spoken to the lawyer."

"Somebody called Crowe? Who the hell is he? She must have gone mad."

"We haven't talked to him yet. I thought it best to have a word with you first. It seemed likely he was some sort of relative or family friend."

"Well, he bloody well isn't!"

"I gathered that."

"You can gather this and all — what's his bloody name won't see a penny of that money."

"According to the lawyer, the will is perfectly legal. *Sound*, he called it." McGuigan had a gift for pouring oil on fire.

"Some shyster! Some kind of Mick or jewboy? My lawyer will sort him out. I'll be on the phone as soon as you're out of here. See him and his client in jail."

"You're upset, sir," McGuigan offered mildly. "Understandably. But you should be careful what you say. It isn't a good idea to slander a lawyer."

"Fucking nonsense. You know how much the Law Society pays out every year to compensate clients for crooked lawyers? Millions!"

Idly, Meldrum wondered about the lawyer, Lester Peters. Not the old Edinburgh type, something slick about him, not hard to imagine him cutting the odd corner. But why would Crowe, whoever he was, need a crooked lawyer to draw up a straightforward will?

Dismissing the idea, Meldrum said, "Thank you anyway for your time. I know this must be hard for you both."

As he stood, Alistair Flett came close. "If she made a will, she was forced."

Meldrum looked down at the flushed face. Like a man lining up for a stroke, he thought.

"Are you talking about duress, sir?"

"Yes! A will that was forced wouldn't be worth the paper it was written on. In fact — in fact — I think she might have said something about being pressured."

"By Antony Crowe?" McGuigan asked.

"Exactly!"

"But I thought you'd never heard of him?"

Flett blinked. "She didn't mention his name, just that this man was pressuring her." Eyes blinking rapidly, he added, "She didn't say what for. But it must have been to make a will. It's obvious, isn't it?"

"I thought you hadn't spoken to your daughter in years," McGuigan said. "Or did I misunderstand you?"

Like a fox dodging a trap, Flett swung from that. "I haven't. But my wife has! She tried to keep it from me, but she talked to Shona. Didn't she tell you she was under pressure? She did, didn't she? Sadie?"

She looked at him with her dazed eyes until he turned away from her.

As they left, he had turned his back as if he couldn't bear to watch her weeping.

CHAPTER
TWENTY-SIX

The house didn't fit someone who had inherited property. Hiding up one of those anonymous roads that strike off across the flat East Lothian landscape with the appearance of being about to turn into a farm track round the first corner, it was a squat cottage with whitewashed peeling walls, and a neglected front garden. A ramshackle building at the side with a rotted wood frame and a badly hung door looked as if it might do service as a garage. It was the last in a line of three similar cottages, the other two looking better cared for with boxes of flowers and tidy shrubs. On its other side, there was the yard of some kind of small factory, surrounded by high fencing topped with razor wire. At its nearest corner, a security camera turned back and forward in search of intruders.

"Good swap," McGuigan said.

"What?"

"A flat in Marchmont for this dump." He looked round and took a deep breath. The air was as fresh and sweet as pegged laundry. On the distant firth, a tanker the size of a toy was making its slow way to Grangemouth. "Nice view, though."

Meldrum, not being a great one for small talk, grunted and led the way up the path.

Before he raised his hand to knock, the door was opened, swinging in to reveal a tall man in carpet slippers. "I saw your car," he said. "I was reading at the window to catch the light. My mother's economical with electricity."

"Mr Crowe?"

"I've been expecting you."

He showed them into a front room as poorly furnished and untidy as might have been predicted from the cottage's exterior.

"Detective Inspector —"

"Meldrum, I know. Put your card away. I saw your picture in the paper. You're investigating the death of Shona Flett. And you are?"

"Detective Sergeant McGuigan."

"And you know who I am." He gathered up a book with a pad of notepaper and a pen on top from the chair by the window and laid all of it on the floor. As they watched, he lifted the chair further into the room and set it down facing the couch. "Take a seat."

As McGuigan hesitated, Meldrum took a seat on the couch. In a later conversation, Crowe would remind Meldrum of this. "It didn't bother you that if you were on the couch and I took the seat, I'd be looking down on you both. I respected that," he would say.

Sitting up as straight as the sagging couch would permit, McGuigan started things off. "We're here to ask you about Shona Flett. You did know her?"

"Is that a serious question?"

114

As McGuigan bristled by his side, Meldrum studied the man opposite. Perhaps four inches shorter than himself, which would make Crowe about six feet. His shoulders were broad and the forearms showing under the rolled up shirtsleeves were thick and corded with muscle. He had broad cheekbones and deep set eyes under heavy brows. The nose had been broken, perhaps more than once. Somebody you'd want to avoid encountering in a dark alley. Not a bad looking man, though. A lived in face. Women probably liked him. His most striking feature was a head of thick black glossy hair, the kind of hair full of life that a certain kind of woman would long to be allowed to stroke. Had Shona Flett been that kind of woman?

"Yes," McGuigan said, after consideration contenting himself with the monosyllable.

"Let me ask you a question then," Crowe said. "You are aware she made me her heir?"

"Yes." The monosyllable even more clipped.

"Doesn't that suggest she knew me? Can we say that's settled? Would you like to ask me a serious question now?"

Meldrum was intrigued. If this display of aggression was some kind of strategy, it was difficult to see what purpose it was intended to serve. It might be intended to mask nervousness, but there was no sign of that kind of discomfort in the man's bearing or in the deep voice with its soft measured emphases. Maybe it was just the way he was. Too much testosterone: not the best impression to give policemen investigating a violent killing.

"We could start with the obvious one," Meldrum said. "What was your relationship with her?"

"Put it another way," Crowe said, "why did she leave me her money?"

"Start with that one, if you want to."

"I have no idea why she did. I'll be honest with you, I was astonished."

"Is that right?" McGuigan asked. "But wasn't it you who found the lawyer?"

"Was it?"

"So Mr Peters told us."

McGuigan's intervention seemed premature to Meldrum, who was a believer in giving a man enough rope to hang himself. It surprised him since he thought of the sergeant as very bright and an astute detective. Perhaps, he thought, the strategy of aggression paid some dividends after all.

"Yes," Crowe said, "I found Lester Peters. Shona told me what she wanted to do — that's where the surprise came in — and that she needed a lawyer to do it. I'd heard his name somewhere, so I tried him."

"It seems an unusual thing to do," McGuigan said stubbornly.

"Because she was leaving me money? You think I should have argued her out of it?"

Meldrum didn't wait for McGuigan to attempt an answer to that. "She was a young woman," he said. "Why did she want to make a will anyway? She was in good health, wasn't she?"

"As far as I know," Crowe said.

"What was the hurry?"

"I've no idea."

"Did you ask her?"

Crowe shrugged. "Can I give you the same answer I gave your colleague? You think I should have argued her out of it?"

"Did you suggest she leave her money to you?" McGuigan asked.

"If I had, I wouldn't have been astonished when she told me."

"So what was your relationship?"

"I met her when I came back from Rome. Seven, coming on eight years ago. If you want to know whether or not we went to bed together, yes, we did."

"You were lovers," McGuigan said, as if double checking.

"I didn't say that. I'm coming on for fifty. It never ceases to surprise me how easily these young women fall into bed. They have the morals of the farmyard. What they call fucking doesn't mean a great deal to them. On that basis, taking her to bed didn't mean I had any great feelings for her. I assumed she felt the same."

"Obviously, though, she took it more seriously," Meldrum said.

"Like I say, I was surprised. By that time, though, we'd known one another for some years. We got on well. Like me, she was interested in religion. Maybe she had some premonition she was going to die."

"Premonition?" McGuigan asked sceptically.

"You've never heard of that? It can happen."

"She told you she was going to die?"

"No." At the denial, Meldrum heard McGuigan suck air through his teeth, a sure signal of his being exasperated. "If she had a premonition, though, it would explain why she wanted to make a will."

"You were there when the will was drawn up?" Meldrum asked.

"I took her to the lawyer. It wouldn't have been right for me to be there when she was instructing him."

"Did you know how much you had been left?"

"Not until Mr Peters read the will to me after her death. Seventy thousand pounds. I had no idea she had so much money."

"But you knew she owned the flat in Marchmont?" McGuigan asked.

"I thought she lodged there. It never occurred to me that she owned it."

"When you first knew her, though, you must have known she owned a dress shop," Meldrum said. Boutique, he corrected himself, remembering Charlotte Tranter's description of her business. It seemed likely that the man she'd described as meeting Shona Flett outside the shop must have been Crowe. To confirm this, he went on, "After all, didn't you go there some evenings to collect her when the shop was closing?"

"Just at first. She left off working there not long after we met."

"You mean she sold up."

"Sold what up?"

"Her half of the business."

"I'm astonished. She told me she was one of the assistants. I wonder why she told me a lie. Why on earth would she do that? You think you know someone . . . Oh, dear. Perhaps she didn't want to embarrass me, so she pretended to be as poor as I was. Do you think that might have been it?"

"What do you do for a living," McGuigan asked, adding, "sir?" as an afterthought.

"How I earn my living?" Crowe rephrased as if to test that he'd understood.

"If you don't mind."

"I think I would. Mind, that is." He waved a hand at the room. "As you can see, I'm staying with my mother. This is her house. Shona visited me here once. Perhaps that's why she left me her money. Perhaps because there wasn't anyone else. After all, she'd quarrelled with her parents."

During the time they'd been talking, the weather must have changed for the interior of the room darkened. Meldrum felt the need of more light but Crowe, it seemed, was content to leave the lamps unlit. This distracted him, and he found it hard to gather his thoughts. He was aware that he should be pressing Crowe, but left it to McGuigan as darkness gathered in the corners of the room; and so it was the detective sergeant who got to the question of where the man had been during the hours when Shona Flett must have been killed and her body disposed of.

"Here," Crowe said.

"Can anyone confirm that?"

"It's not much of an alibi, you mean? Not being able to prove you were somewhere else must be one of the dangers of innocence. The guilty probably manage things better."

"Does that mean no one can confirm you were here?"

"There's always my mother."

"Could we have a word with her, please?"

"For what it's worth," Crowe said, and got up.

He came back with an elderly woman, who was still in a dressing gown, either because she had never got round to putting clothes on or because she had been taking a nap and been fetched out of bed. Again, Meldrum left the questioning to McGuigan, whose irritation at being left unsupported he could sense. It was routine stuff, however, apart from the fact that Crowe made no more effort than Meldrum to contribute. She quickly supported the claim that her son had been at home all that day and hadn't left the house during the night. Before she was asked, she claimed to be a poor sleeper who would certainly have heard if he'd tried to leave. As confirmation, again without being asked, she offered that her bedroom was at the end of the house next to the garage and that she would have been bound to hear it if the car had been started. As this familiar process went on, Meldrum's thoughts wandered to his daughter Betty and his grandson until, realising what he was doing, with a stab of something like fear he forced himself to pay attention.

At last, it was over.

Just at the moment of escape, about to step out on to the path, Meldrum found Crowe leaning over to him and saying in a soft confidential voice which seemed intended to exclude the sergeant, "What mother wouldn't lie for her son? And so you didn't waste your energy on it. You are a remarkable man."

CHAPTER
TWENTY-SEVEN

As was often the way, luck rather than persistence finally turned up the place where Michael Thorne ate his evening meals. By this time, it had been suggested to Meldrum that the search was taking up more time than it was worth. An alternative idea had been mooted that the old man might have regularly brought in a carry out and eaten it on his own in his flat. No shortage of such places round about. He could have had his pick of Italian, Mexican, Chinese, Thai, Spanish. Spoiled for choice, why would anyone eat out? Another suggestion by the mutinous detective trio was that perhaps his son Colin Halliday fed him each evening. Asking Halliday, who denied either knowing or caring where his father had eaten, eliminated that possibility. Showing the old man's photograph around the carry out places had brought the team nothing except a change of scene. And then Houston had announced that if he didn't take his wife out for their twentieth anniversary she was going to leave him, which touched a raw nerve with Meldrum who, to everyone's astonishment, gave him the evening off.

This was the same evening, as it happened, on which the mystery was solved. MacIntosh spotted a fish and chip shop up a lane. Shown the photograph of Michael Thorne, the sallow proprietor told him, "Like clockwork every night. Mostly a fish supper, sometimes a pie supper or a white pudding supper, occasionally, not very often, maybe when he wasn't hungry, he'd just have a spring roll supper. Other times, he'd have a round pie supper or a steak pie supper. That man loved his suppers."

Meanwhile Houston was having his own moment of triumph. "It would never have occurred to me in a million years," he repeated next day. "Who'd have thought an old git like Thorne living like a down and out would go to a place like that?"

"Wonder they let you in," Sharkey said sourly. After so much pavement pounding, his sense of humour had failed him over an accidental discovery.

"It was our anniversary," Houston pointed out reasonably. "And the wife scrubs up very nicely."

"What the hell made you show the waiter the photo?"

"It was in my wallet."

"Come on!"

After some more or less skilful probing, the truth came out. "The wife had been giving me a hard time. Fuck me, I take her out to this hotel. Spend a fortune on a meal, and then when we adjourn to the bar, she starts nagging about how little I've been home. It's the job, I tell her. Fuck the job, she says. She's had one drink too many. You mean the one that pays for all this? I ask her. I'm getting my wallet out to pay. I've got it in the inside jacket pocket, and here I pull the photo out with it. Must have put them both in by mistake when I transferred the wallet from my other jacket. So I show it to the waiter — just for devilment, I was trying to wind her up. When the guy recognised it," declared Houston, a burly man with a neck like a bull, "you could have knocked me down with a feather."

CHAPTER
TWENTY-EIGHT

Sipping at his whisky, Meldrum watched McGuigan, a stickler for the rules, gloomily working his way down a fresh orange.

They'd already interviewed the waiter who'd identified for the second time a photograph of Michael Thorne. "We cried him the Laird o' Cockpen," he'd said. Reassured that they were interested in murder, not in vice, he relaxed and went on, "With the emphasis on *cock*. Always left with a woman, get it? How often? I'd just be guessing, couple of times a month, maybe more? But for years, like, back and forward. When I came here, he was pointed out to me — the Laird o' Cockpen. Didn't look as if he'd two pennies to rub together, but the girls he went away with weren't cheap. And they must have been happy enough, for he went with the same ones a few times."

"Which ones?"

"I couldn't give you names and addresses!" Seeing how badly his snort of laughter went down with McGuigan, he hurried on, "I'd nothing to do with them! I could give you some first names. At least, the ones they offer the men who buy them a drink. Let me think." And in a rush he came out with a string of names. "Sadie, Francine, Marie, Petra."

"You've a good memory," Meldrum said.

"*And* I'm about ready to pack it in here. If you want to come in one night, I'll point them out. Should be at least one of them around."

It had struck Meldrum that spending an evening in a hotel bar would be better than brooding in his flat. In the event, however, as he should have known, time spent with McGuigan had become unpleasant for them both. It got worse when the waiter bent over to whisper, "Marie" and discreetly indicated a woman alone in a corner whom Meldrum recognised. She was the whore whose bed he had wakened in twice after a bout of binge drinking.

When the two detectives sat themselves at her table, however, she was shrewd enough to give no sign of recognition. Indeed, it was McGuigan who effortlessly kept her attention. Whichever of them asked a question, it was the detective sergeant she looked at as she answered, eyes widening, voice a little husky. If they had been prospective clients, there would have been no doubt as to which she would have preferred. It wasn't the first time Meldrum had observed the sergeant's effect on women. No chance, he thought with a touch of grim amusement, noting McGuigan's frozen-faced disdain.

Given the same reassurance that it was death not commercial sex they were investigating, she talked freely. "You know what they called him? Aye, the Laird.

Something about him, the style of him, even though his trouser cuffs were frayed."

"Did you go with him?" Meldrum asked.

Eyes fixed on McGuigan, she said in a confidential murmur, "Good shoes even if they were old, that was another thing. I was told when I started on this game, take a look at a punter's shoes."

"So you went with him?"

"First time, I nearly told him to bugger off, but apart from him the place was dead. One of those nights. Before I said yes, I leaned over and took a sniff. He looked like one of those old guys who'd smell a bit. I can't be doing with that." She tried a smile on McGuigan. "I think he'd had a bath special like."

"Get on with it," he said.

"And he was all right, paid up, no problem. And he could get it up. Not like some of the younger ones." She licked a tongue across her lips. "Didn't have to suck him or anything. Got his end away, dressed and said thank you like a gentleman. Tell you, I've had a lot worse."

"And you saw him again?"

"He was in here a few times."

"And?"

"Not every time. I think he liked a change. And sometimes I'd already have made an arrangement."

"Would you say you got to know him?" Meldrum asked.

"He wasn't the kind to tell you his life story, if that's what you mean."

"Never lie on afterwards and talk for a wee while?"

"Once they've shot their load most punters can't wait to get away." This time her eyes did slide round to hold Meldrum's. "Anyway, you know what they say, time's money."

"Ever talk about his family?"

"I did have a guy talked all the time about his mother." A whore with a heart of gold after all, Meldrum thought. "But that wasn't the old fellow's style."

"Never talked about his past at all?"

"No."

"I think he must have talked about something, Marie. We know he lived alone. People that live alone need to talk. Sometimes when they get started they can't stop. They'll tell you about who they're fighting with, any trouble they're having, all kinds of stuff."

"He wasn't like that."

"You're telling me he didn't say anything even when you were in the bar having a drink?"

"Oh, he'd talk a bit then."

"What about?"

She thought for a moment, putting her chin on her hand. "One time he told me about Billy Graham. I'd no idea who he was on about, so he told me. He'd seen him at a rally in the Kelvin Hall in Glasgow. About all the folk getting up and going down to the front to get converted. I asked him if he'd gone down and he gave a wee smile and said he didn't have to."

Case bloody solved, Meldrum thought, Billy did it.

McGuigan, too, had had enough. "Who else did he go with?" And when she hesitated, "Come on, we know the names. Just confirm them for us."

It turned out, however, that she could put a name to fewer of the women than the waiter, only two first names, both of which they already had.

Ready to give up, Meldrum was easing back his chair when she said, "Oh, there was one thing. Used to get on my tits. When he was, you know, doing it, when he was excited, he'd say a name. I didn't mind that it wasn't mine, why the hell should it be? But the one he shouted was my grandmother's name and that didn't feel right — it upset me. Got so I told him to stop doing it, but it was as if he couldn't help himself."

"What name was that?"

"Bridget."

As soon as she said the name, Meldrum knew he'd heard it before in connection with Michael Thorne. He'd always had a good memory. Like a filing cabinet. But when he needed it now the drawers were empty. Pulling them out, slamming them back, he struggled to show nothing of his distress. To make matters worse, he could see that whatever the connection was McGuigan had just made it.

CHAPTER
TWENTY-NINE

The simplest thing would have been to ask McGuigan about this "Bridget". Since it might be important, it would also have been the professional thing to do. Rather than show weakness, however, Meldrum chose to wait, assuming that McGuigan would bring it up himself and in doing so probably give the clue that was needed. As if the sergeant had somehow understood this, he said nothing about it; and Meldrum might have been forced at last by common sense or conscience to raise the matter himself if it had not been for a journalist calling an awkward question from the back row of a press conference. As he answered on autopilot, Meldrum looked at the questioner and the man's name came into his head without effort. Chris Eastwood. Six foot tall and at a guess one hundred and thirty pounds soaking wet. Narrow shoulders, narrow face. Lugubrious expression, a fag behind his ear. "A tall thin streak of misery, stinking of cigarettes." Who'd said that? The answer came to him as the conference broke up.

Cornering Eastwood, he asked, "Where do you get off going to see Shona Flett's parents and telling them she was dead?" He'd never seen a trapped weasel, but from the man's grimace he knew he'd guessed right.

"Her father's furious with you. He couldn't remember your name, but I'll pass it on to him so he can do something about it. All that stuff about her being naked, you're a real cunt, aren't you?"

From this unpromising start, the journalist contrived a conversation in a local pub, which ended with him putting Meldrum in his debt. Practising that kind of horse-trading must have been part of his survival kit, and he was very good at it. It began with him sliding away from the Shona Flett difficulty by asking, "You've got Michael Thorne on your plate as well, haven't you? You knew he was a priest?"

"A minister. Get your facts right."

"*Before* he was a minister. He was a priest. Here, in Edinburgh."

The ancient scandal Eastwood uncovered had happened fifty years earlier, long before his time. His father, a sub editor in his day, in retirement confined his reading to sports and stock market reports, and had only just provided him with the details after coming across an item on Thorne by accident. Although Meldrum spoke to the father later, he added nothing to the account that his son had given. Whatever else he might be, Eastwood was a professional who could wring out a source.

In the late nineteen fifties, Michael Thorne had been a young priest in an Edinburgh parish. Since he was devout, conscientious and very bright, he was a tip for the future, one to watch, a bishop in the making and who knew what after that? And then one fine day it came out he was having an affair with a twenty-year-old parishioner. "The girl's father was fierce on keeping her and her six sisters innocent," Eastwood said. "And Thorne had been picked out for a priest from when he was a ten-year-old. So one was as naïve as the other. They went to bed — maybe a couple of times, maybe only once — and the girl missed her period. He got such a fright, he went straight to his superior. Nobody was going to give him a pat on the back — but he wasn't the first priest to be in that predicament. He was only twenty-three, and if some woman threw herself at him . . ." Eastwood shrugged and grinned. "Hasn't it always been Eve's fault? Anyway, the bishop thought well of him, and no one likes to see talent wasted, so he was told things could be sorted out. He'd have to dump the girl, of course, never clap eyes on her from that moment on. The baby could be adopted. Or maybe the girl's mother would bring the baby up as her own. It wouldn't be the first time that a child had been brought up thinking its mother was its sister. Meantime, he'd be sent off to a monastery for a bit to sort himself out. After that, he could pick up where he left off."

"He must have stopped being a priest at some point," Meldrum said. "By the time he married his second wife he was a Pentecostal minister."

"We'll get to that. My father had sniffed out all this stuff about the priest and the parishioner. He thought it was a good story, but the editor killed it. It annoyed him enough to keep an eye out for Thorne. He said to me, if ever the bastard got to be Pope I was going to nail him." He gave the same foxy grin. "Remind you of anybody?"

132

"Aye, you're a chip off the old block."

"My father didn't know whether he went to a monastery or wherever, but he turned up again in Edinburgh two years later. Large as life and still looking as though he'd go a long way in the Church. My father, just for himself, a wee bit of private enterprise, nothing to do with the paper, decided he'd see what had happened to the girl while lover boy was away. Turned out she'd had the baby, but it wasn't adopted and her mother didn't take it in either, maybe the old father put his foot down. The wee one had been put in a Home, run by some order of nuns. And that was that. A few years went by, end of story, my father thought. Only it wasn't. By the time my father learned the next bit, it was too late. Thorne had given up the priesthood and slipped away — so it was all hushed up, and my father never got his story into print." He paused as if thinking.

A veteran of interviews, Meldrum recognised when an informant, like a seal being thrown a fish, needed the encouragement of a prompt. "What happened?" he asked.

"The dog went back to its vomit."

"What does that mean?"

"Turns out he couldn't keep away from the woman. He was no sooner back in Edinburgh than they were at it again. He was smart, though, and it took a while before they were caught."

"So he was kicked out of the priesthood?"

Eastwood took the cigarette out from behind his ear, sniffed at it and put it back. "Nanny state. Pint doesn't taste the same without a fag," he said. "My father didn't know. Again it wasn't ever in the papers. Thorne and the woman disappeared out of the city, presumably together. This time it *was* the end of the story, at least as far as the old man was concerned."

"Your father tell you the woman's name?"

"Oh, yes. He talked to her a couple of times. My father wasn't much for the women, but he remembered her all right. Red hair, cream complexion. Not exactly a beauty. But there was something about her. Way he put it, she'd give a dead man a stiff prick."

CHAPTER
THIRTY

"Bridget," Meldrum said. "Bridget O'Neill. Mrs Halliday mentioned Bridget as the name of the woman who took her first husband, Thorne, away from her. And the prostitute in the hotel said Thorne persisted in calling her Bridget when he was in bed with her. A hack called Chris Eastwood provided the O'Neill bit. I spotted him at the press conference."

"That was lucky," McGuigan said.

"You make your own luck," Meldrum said smugly.

The journey from Edinburgh to Glasgow should only have taken them an hour. As usual, however, the M8 was plagued by roadworks and they crawled in second gear for miles. Even once they'd passed the Glasgow boundary, traffic jammed after junction fifteen. It was a relief to get off the motorway and settle down to the long slog from red light to red light along Great Western Road. At Anniesland Cross, they turned along the Switchback, the road rising and falling as they headed for Bearsden.

"According to the map, it's off on the right hand side."

McGuigan grunted at the advice, passed a couple of road ends and seemed to choose the next one on impulse. They found themselves in an estate of neat identical bungalows fronted by clipped hedges, cherry trees and rose bushes. It didn't help that only the occasional one bothered to show a number, though many had been named. The one they were seeking announced itself as SUILVEN, the name burned into a pine board.

The man who came to the door was red-faced, eighty plus, with a round cannon-ball belly he was tall enough to carry off under a grey woollen cardigan. Eyes narrow with suspicion, while they identified themselves and he admitted reluctantly to being Frank O'Neill, he kept them on the front doorstep. As they spoke, Meldrum felt his nose blocking with the heavy mingled scents of furniture polish from the hall and roses lining the path behind them. At mention of his daughter's name, he looked around as if a neighbour might be spying from behind one of the shorn hedges and waved them inside.

Leaning heavily on a stick, he took them through into a sun-filled conservatory at the back of the house. There was a set of comfortable cane chairs, but he placed them round a small table set for lunch, laid his stick against the wall and asked why they were there.

"We're investigating the murder of Michael Thorne," Meldrum explained.

"Never heard of him."

"No point in taking that line, sir," Meldrum said. "We know about him and your daughter."

"I had seven daughters," O'Neill said. "Two of them became nuns. One married a bank manager. One

136

married an electrician with his own business. One lives here and looks after me."

"I make that five not seven," McGuigan said.

"One defied me and married a weed of a man. I only have four grandchildren."

McGuigan shook his head impatiently. "What about Bridget?"

"She's dead."

"When did she die?" Meldrum asked.

"A long time ago."

"Could you be more precise?"

"1956."

"I don't think so. We know that she was alive after that."

The old man frowned. His lips came together in a thin bloodless line. "Dead to me," he said. "On the sixteenth of February, 1956, at half four in the afternoon, when she told me she was pregnant. If you want to know anything about her, you've come to the wrong door. I haven't spoken to her in more than forty years, I haven't seen her, I don't know anything about her. You've had your journey for nothing."

"So you don't know where she is now?" Meldrum asked.

O'Neill didn't bother to acknowledge the obvious.

"I should say to you," Meldrum persisted, "that this is a murder enquiry. It wouldn't be a good idea to deliberately withhold information."

"Are you trying to frighten me?"

"I'm just explaining the situation."

"Go on explaining it in that tone, and I'll be putting in a complaint to your superiors. I might do it anyway."

"If you feel you have to," Meldrum said.

O'Neill stood up ready to show them out. As McGuigan followed his example, Meldrum, still seated, asked, "When you say you've four grandchildren, does that include Bridget's child?"

"It does not."

"You know she had the child?"

"I think you should go."

"Before we do, would you tell us where you were on the tenth of the month?"

"Why would you ask me that?" And then before Meldrum could answer, O'Neill snorted, "Was that when this murder of yours happened? God almighty, have you taken leave of your senses?"

"There are questions we have to ask."

"It's ridiculous!"

"From what you've told us," Meldrum said, "it's obvious that you still feel strongly about what happened with Michael Thorne and your daughter."

"I'm eighty-five. I have a bad leg. It *hurts* when I walk. So you're trying to suggest I got in my car, which by the way I can't drive any more, and went to Edinburgh to find this Thorne whom I haven't seen hilt nor hair of for forty years and killed him. How did I do it? Did I kick him to death with my bad leg? You didn't say, did you?"

"You're right, I didn't say," Meldrum said, "but I didn't say anything about him being killed in Edinburgh either."

CHAPTER
THIRTY-ONE

Cadoc couldn't stop shivering.

"I've got flu," he complained.

"I don't think so," the Convenor said. "I'd call it a panic attack."

Cadoc stared gloomily at the single wan bar of the electric fire, which provided the only heating in the large, high-ceilinged front room of the Marchmont flat.

"The cold in this place is killing me."

The Convenor hadn't taken his coat off. Lounging in its warmth, he stared at the younger man. "Putting up with hardship is part of your training. You've picked a bad time to start whining. Have you forgotten what happened to Bryd?"

"Shona." The name came out like a groan of pain.

"They mutilated her body."

"I know."

"The only thing between you with your throat cut and your prick cut off is discipline. All the training we've done is about that, always has been, right from the beginning."

"But we're not a group any more!"

"I think we are."

"The other two are hidden up in the hills. Who's going to find them there? But I'm alone here. If they knew about Shona, they know about me. They know I'm here. I lie awake through there listening all night, waiting for the door to open." Like a child, he put his fingertips over his mouth. "I can't go on."

"And me? Have you anything to say about me? Am I safe too? Are you the only one in danger?"

"I didn't say that." He visibly gathered courage to add, "But maybe they *don't* know where you live. None of us ever did."

"So here you are on your own. Poor you." He smiled. "At least you have food to eat."

Cadoc stared at him in dismay. "What do you mean? I thought there was food in the house."

"It turns out when they looked there wasn't."

"My God, what will they do?"

"Hold out. Their discipline is maybe better than yours."

"But they'll need food!"

"And you'll take it to them tomorrow. Fill the boot of your car and make sure you aren't followed. Same routine I gave you when you took them there. You remember it?"

Cadoc flushed and stared at him. The Convenor laughed and took a sheet of paper from his pocket and handed it across. "No, I didn't think you would. I've written out the route again. Memorise before you start."

"I won't get there till late. I have my work and then I'll need to get the food."

"Not locally."

"No."

"They'll have all tonight and tomorrow."

"They'll manage. Women know how to endure. The stronger sex, you've heard that? And you won't just be taking food. Tell them we aren't going to sit and wait for the enemy to come to us. Tell them, it's our turn now."

"To do what?" The question came in a reedy whisper.

"Stand up!"

Cadoc stumbled to his feet.

"Hands by your sides."

The Convenor slapped first one side of the younger man's face then the other.

"Keep your hands down! Look at me! Look at me! Look at me!"

Methodically for five minutes the blows came. Cadoc was wide eyed with shock as it went on and on, seemingly forever.

When it stopped, the Convenor sat down again. Trembling, Cadoc remained standing, seemingly unconscious of the thin trickle of blood that ran from the corner of his mouth, until the voice commanded, "Sit down!"

Slowly the Convenor unbuttoned his coat and let it fall open. "That warmed me up," he said pleasantly.

Still dazed, Cadoc sat for a moment and then whispered, "Will you stay tonight?"

"That won't be possible." He put his hand under his jacket and slid out a small revolver. "I brought you this. Put it under your pillow and you'll sleep."

Cadoc looked at it in fright. "I don't know how to use it. I've never held a gun in my life."

"I'll show you before I go. It's not difficult. Safety catch off. It's loaded. Aim it as if you were pointing at the target. Wait as long as you can. Pull the trigger. Your only problem should be disposing of the body." He smiled. "If it's as cold in here as you imagine, it should keep till my next visit."

Cadoc took the gun from him and cradled it against his chest. When he started crying, it began as little snuffling gasps, which gradually transformed into sobs that shook him from head to foot.

"I'm sorry," he said. "I'm sorry. But you don't understand. No one can understand what it means to kill your father."

"Oh, I think I could try," the Convenor said. "It's a solemn thing."

"A terrible thing!"

"But didn't I show you proof?" He waited not willing to say more until the little nod of assent was given. "That old man was part of it. Like so many others who look unimportant and have the future of the world in their hands. Didn't he have to be stopped?"

Softly, "Yes," the sobbing slowing, quietening.

"And won't we do what else has to be done? Isn't it time to deal with them, the ones crouching in the dark?" He leaned forward and laid his hand on the younger man's knee. "You've done well. Everything will be all right." The hand pressing gently now on the thigh. "Calm yourself." Rubbing up and down the thigh. "It's a shame that you've been so cold. Now we'll fix that." Rubbing, rubbing. "There's more than one way of getting warm."

CHAPTER
THIRTY-TWO

It occurred to Meldrum, as he sat sipping black coffee and waiting for the morning conference, that there might be something pitiable about Michael Thorne. If all they'd heard was true, meeting a woman of extraordinary sexual attractiveness had altered his life. He'd fallen in love with her as a young priest, fathered a child, given up his vocation, found another, got married, and for a second time lost everything for the same woman. Solitary at the end of his life, Meldrum could picture him going out and bringing back a fish supper to eat on his own. He didn't find this hard to envisage, since it was something he often did himself. Afterwards, on some evenings, they had learned Thorne would go out and drink alone, pick up a prostitute and, sometimes, it seemed, as he neared a climax, would call out the name of the woman he'd first met a lifetime earlier. The sequence struck Meldrum as sad, but he wasn't even slightly tempted to share this perception with McGuigan, whom he suspected might meet it by looking blank, unsympathetic or contemptuous. After all, he wasn't even sure how the DS felt about fish suppers.

They were all in the conference room waiting. As the session went on, his sense of frustration made a growing irritability hard to conceal. It didn't help that he had to incline his head to catch sight of DC Petrie, who as usual had managed the trick of being half concealed behind someone else.

"What about the lists, Donald?" he asked

Convinced the murders of Thorne and Shona Flett were connected by more than the chance that Colin Halliday was the son of one and had been the lodger of the other, he'd put DC Petrie on to examining the lists of students in Colin Halliday's classes and seminar groups. It had seemed worth checking since neighbours had described one of the women at the Halliday flat as being young, but he'd done it without much hope anything would come of it.

"Nothing really. I got a list from the office at the college, but classes aren't started yet."

"He was taking a class when we went to see him," McGuigan said, looking at Meldrum for confirmation.

"I'm just telling you what they told me in the office." Petrie hesitated. "Right enough, she did say there are catch up groups and other stuff going on. Before the year proper gets going."

"Did you check on them then?" Meldrum asked. "That must have been what Halliday was involved with when we saw him. Anyone who should have been at these groups who hasn't put in an appearance?"

"I didn't think. I mean if the year hadn't started . . ."

The words "thick", "idle" and "bastard" occurred to Meldrum, but when McGuigan only too audibly muttered, "Fuck's sake", he contented himself by suggesting that the sergeant go back himself and check it out. Not the best way to build a happy squad, but divide and conquer wasn't a bad management principle either. For the rest, he recycled tasks, ordered re-interviews, put people on to digging into the backgrounds of the two victims and Shona Flett's heir Antony Crowe. It was all reasonable police work, but it lacked direction and he had nothing to offer by way of breaking the jam. Like the divide and conquer principle, it was unworthy of the way he'd run every previous investigation in which he'd been involved. If he hadn't been aware of that in his guts, he would have known from the subtle change he sensed in the team's attitude to him. The ground was moving under his feet, but he had been at this game too long not to be able to fake it at least for a time.

CHAPTER
THIRTY-THREE

By the time he got to the youngest one, Meldrum was sick of Frank O'Neill's daughters. The spinster daughter who stayed in Bearsden with her father had hated the two policemen at first sight. They had gone to her workplace and that interview had ended with her, too, threatening to report them to their superiors, adding as her own refinement the sheer unreasonableness of imagining a man like her father capable of any wrongdoing. In her book, questioning him amounted to something close to sacrilege. Driving back to Glasgow, McGuigan had exclaimed, "Religion's turned that one's head," which startled Meldrum, who privately regarded his colleague as having displayed on occasion a touch of the same problem.

Two of the daughters were nuns in closed orders. Interestingly, they were the two who came next after Bridget, who'd been the first born, and Meldrum wondered if her sin had put them under pressure conspicuously to take a different path. They had managed interviews with the daughter who had married the bank manager and the one who had been snapped up by the electrician "with his own business." No threats from either, but a total unhelpfulness as they peeped at the detectives over the wall of their respectability.

All of which made for an expectation as they rolled along through a scheme of small council houses in Tranent that the last and youngest of the brood would be as unforthcoming as her siblings.

Siobhan Riordan came as a pleasant surprise. She had no inhibitions about the past or present of her family. Once they'd explained themselves, her first reaction was surprise that her father had mentioned her at all.

"He doesn't even have my address," she said.

"We got it from Mrs Martin, your sister," Meldrum explained.

"Right. How is she then?"

"She seemed fine," McGuigan said dismissively.

"Bank must be doing well." She laughed showing even white teeth. Hair dyed professionally to a light brown with golden streaks, she looked younger than the fifty-year-old they'd expected; if her father had got it right, marriage to what he'd called "a weed of a man" wasn't usually good for the looks. In fact, she was a handsome woman, if too stout. Meldrum could see a strong family resemblance to her father and sisters, though somewhat disguised in her case by her readiness to smile. "So you've seen all of my sisters?"

"No," Meldrum admitted. "It didn't seem the two in the convent would have much to say to us."

"Not without breaking their vows! I was only a child when Clare and Mary took them. You know I'm the youngest?"

"Yes."

"Poor Bridget," she said. "That fellow Michael Thorne ruined her life. I told her that."

"When did you do that?" McGuigan asked sharply.

She blinked at him, then smiled. "Oh, not when I was a child! I was only little when she had all her trouble about being pregnant. After that she disappeared out of our lives. But she came back into mine!"

"When would that be?" asked Meldrum, almost repeating the earlier question.

"I was married, and having my own trouble with my father by then. He'd cut me off because I married a Protestant." Again she gave that full chuckling laugh at their look of confusion. "Mrs Riordan? is that what you're thinking? Well, I'll tell you worse than that. My husband's name's Malachi, though he calls himself Malkie. He gave up being a Catholic on his sixteenth birthday when he went to a priest to ask about some problems of faith and was sent away with a flea in his ear. If he'd gone to a better priest, he'd still be a Catholic I tell him. But the fool told him it wasn't for the likes of him, a poor boy from a poor family, to be troubling his head with that stuff. Malkie has a great sense of himself, and that was it." She laughed again. "I hear you policemen are all Masons. If Malkie was here he'd be able to give you the handshake. When he started on his own as a joiner — this was when we lived in Glasgow — as soon as they heard his name, half of the firms wouldn't give him a chance and the other half would ask which parish he went to — and then they'd put him to the door as well! In self-defence, he joined the Masons or we'd have been starving."

Meldrum, who had been following politely, felt constrained to ask at her first pause, "You were going to tell us about your sister Bridget?"

"I was so taken aback. There was a knock at the door one morning and there she was. Did I say we were in Glasgow then, a house in Barmulloch? She'd traced me through our wedding certificate and then through Malkie's mother, who still lived in Edinburgh. I was in tears, I tell you, I'm not ashamed to admit it. That was after she told me who she was, for I didn't recognise her. She had a cup of tea and fussed over the little one, my first baby. And she asked about my father and the others, and I told her what I knew for, as I said, I'd had my own difficulties. She went over her whole story with me, about the baby she'd had and how it had been taken from her and sent to a Home and how she'd been ill for a time and then about how that man had come looking for her again and about him leaving the priesthood. But after he'd done that he couldn't cope, she told me, for he was meant to be a priest. That's what broke us up, she said. But then she told me that she was seeing Michael Thorne *again*!" She shook her head. "But when she told me he was married — and some kind of minister — and that he wanted to leave his wife for her! That's when I told her, he's been the ruin of you once, don't let it happen again." She fell silent. "You know what she said to me?"

As he waited, Meldrum was struck by the look of sadness that had settled upon her.

150

"What did she say?"

" 'It's me that's ruined him', she said."

It seemed to Meldrum that might be near the truth.

As if she had sensed his thoughts, Siobhan Riordan said, "*He* was the *man. He* was the *priest.* Whose fault was it, if it wasn't his?" As quickly as it had come, the fierceness drained from her. "That's what I told her. I didn't miss her and hit the wall. I should have put it better, but it all came on me suddenly. I'd opened the door and there she was. The long-lost sister. And me with my head full of catching the bus down into Springburn for the shops. I'd no time to think it over or to plan what I would say or to talk to somebody about it. There were just those few hours that one morning. I wasn't to know that's all I would have. I sometimes feel it was all my fault."

"What was?" McGuigan asked.

Involuntarily, Meldrum looked at the sergeant, who wasn't usually slow on the uptake.

Siobhan Riordan blinked as if in surprise. "That I didn't persuade her to have nothing more to do with him. I've thought since, why did she come to see me? There must have been a bit of her that wasn't sure. Maybe if I'd known what to say to her, things might have been different. I made a hash of it, she got angry with me, and when she left I was in no doubt she was going to go away again with him. I never found out, of course. Before she left, I made her promise to write to me. But when Malkie came in at night, he said, that's the last you'll hear from her. We'd a stand up fight over that, but he was right. And now you tell me Michael

Thorne's been murdered. Was she with him when it happened? For God's sake, don't tell me it was her!"

She had a quick mind and a quick tongue. Actually holding up his hand as if to stem the flow of her words and thoughts, Meldrum said, "She wasn't there."

"Thank God for that!"

"He was living alone when he was killed," Meldrum said. "They'd split up."

"That's hard to believe. After he'd come looking for her. And she was crazy about him."

McGuigan frowned at her. He'd made it plain to Meldrum that in his opinion a motive for the old man's death would be found not in his past but among the prostitutes he'd frequented. A grunt had been Meldrum's response, and then he'd led them both on the round of the daughters. Now, "Maybe she's dead," McGuigan said flatly.

"And maybe she isn't!" the woman said defiantly.

Meldrum decided it was time to call a halt. He thanked her and got to his feet.

As they were going out of the front door, she caught Meldrum by his sleeve.

"I don't believe she's dead," she said, her voice low as if she wanted only him to hear. "At least she wasn't five years ago."

"What makes you think that?" Meldrum asked quietly.

"I saw her on the other side of the street in Princes Street in Edinburgh. Just for a moment, but I knew it was her. There was too much traffic, and by the time I got across she'd gone. I thought she might have gone into the Gardens and so I went down and walked round it for a long time. It wasn't any use. Full of people, none of them her."

CHAPTER
THIRTY-FOUR

"Explain that to me again," Meldrum said too quietly.

They were on their way back to Edinburgh. As usual McGuigan was driving, and as he answered he kept his eyes fixed on the road ahead.

"I got the names, and I passed them to Billy Petrie."

"I asked you to check them yourself."

"I did. I did what he should have done. I went to the office and asked about the classes that were happening before the term started. I found the lecturers who were involved and gave their names to Billy. He should have checked them out by now."

Meldrum felt a vein flickering under his eye. "I always thought," he said in the same quiet voice, "that it didn't matter what else you were, you were a good cop."

"You're saying I'm not?"

"I'm saying that was a lazy fuckup's way of going about things."

"I resent that."

"What would you call it?"

McGuigan's face was expressionless, his voice no louder than Meldrum's, but the speedometer needle crept up towards ninety.

"I can't be in two places at once. You wanted to talk to this Bridget O'Neill's sisters. Maybe I'd have been better talking to the lecturers, but it wasn't me who thought the sisters were important."

Meldrum didn't answer. There was no more conversation until suddenly Meldrum asked, "Where the fuck do you think you're going?"

McGuigan was startled, either by the question or the second expletive. Meldrum hardly ever swore. Before he could respond, Meldrum said, "Take the next left . . . Straight on . . . Take a right." And so it went on in a flat monotone till at one instruction, McGuigan burst out, "The College? Why not say so? Just say that's where you want. I know how to get to the fucking College."

"No need to swear," Meldrum said disapprovingly.

The list was a short one. Although many lecturers were working in the College before the term began, only half a dozen were involved with student groups. Meldrum's eye was caught by one name in particular.

"You didn't think it worth while to have a word with Colin Halliday at least?"

"There would be more pressure on him, if he saw Petrie first and then had a second visit."

"And what did he say to Petrie?"

"I haven't seen Petrie."

Meldrum contented himself with a grunt.

In fact, that afternoon they paid two visits to Halliday. In between, they talked to three other lecturers on the list. The others were out of the building.

Halliday looked up in surprise when they appeared for the second time at his office door.

"Yes?"

Meldrum came in and took a seat. His pace was deliberate and McGuigan matched it as he took another.

"We've been talking to a colleague of yours. A Mr Lawrence."

"David, yes, he's in the maths department."

"That's the one. Like yourself, he's got a group he's seeing at the moment. One of them stopped coming, which has irritated him. A girl called Keeley Robertson. Have you heard of her?"

It wasn't a long pause, but it was a pause where none should have been. It was enough to let Meldrum know that the young man had to calculate his answer to what should have been a simple matter of fact.

"She was in my first year class last session."

"You were meeting with a group when we were here before. Was Miss Robertson part of it?"

"Yes, she would have been there."

"And for the last few days?"

"You're right. She wasn't here last time."

McGuigan leaned forward. "Can you explain why you said to us before that no one was missing?"

Startlingly, Halliday laughed with what seemed to be genuine amusement. "Missing because of one or two absences? I don't suppose you've ever been a student. Believe me, they aren't that conscientious!"

"That's not," McGuigan said, "the way your colleague looked at it. Yes, he said normally they might

156

skip a class, but they had an obligation to attend these groups or let the office know. He was concerned enough to check, but she hadn't phoned in with any explanation for not being at class."

"Oh, dear," Halliday said. "I'm afraid that isn't quite the way it is. How can I put this? She's a very pretty girl. And David Lawrence has an eye for a pretty girl."

"Are you suggesting he's having an affair with her?"

"As for that," Halliday said, "I have no idea at all."

CHAPTER THIRTY-FIVE

"If it had been me," McGuigan said, "I'd have asked this guy Lawrence if he was sleeping with the girl."

"We don't know she's the one we're after."

They'd gone back to the office in the College and got Keeley Robertson's address. Despite his hopes, it came as no surprise that he didn't recognise it. Too much to hope for that she might have given the address of Colin Halliday's flat. All the same, he had a strong instinct that this might be the young girl who had been seen there by neighbors.

"But wouldn't it have been worth talking to Lawrence again?" McGuigan had a habit of not letting go easily, useful to a detective in most instances, but not always welcome.

Meldrum didn't answer or speak again until they were pulling up outside the house in North Berwick. "Halliday's a born liar. Can't you tell?" He was out of the car before McGuigan could respond.

It had taken them under an hour to get to the coastal town. Waiting on the step, they could smell the freshness of salt on the wind.

Meldrum had noticed that many men seemed to plateau and keep the same looks for twenty years; some well fed, comfortable retirees looked fresh for decades more; a lucky few into old age, some till the day they died; at some point, though, for most, one illness too many or a bereavement caused a collapse into lines and gauntness as if the picture in the attic had fallen off the wall. It wasn't, then, always easy to estimate age. Despite which, taking account at a glance of the scanty white hair, the thin lips, a joyless lack of energy in the face, he was sure Keeley Robertson's father, giving him all the benefit of the doubt, had to be nearer seventy than sixty, on the old side to have a nineteen-year-old daughter.

"I don't know why you are looking for her here," he said, sounding irritable rather than concerned.

"This is the address she gave the College."

"It doesn't make sense. She hasn't lived here for ten years."

"It's the only address they have."

"So that's why . . . Stuff did come for her. I didn't even open it. Just wrote her mother's address on it and put it back in the box."

"She lives with her mother?" Meldrum asked.

"If she doesn't, I don't know where she does. When her mother went off, she took the child with her."

Although he had allowed them in and closed the door behind them, he hadn't invited them into the front room, and so they stood as an awkward group in the hall.

"If you could let us have your wife's address?"

He turned and they watched him start to climb the stairs. After a few steps, he swung round and came down again.

"You'll stay here?"

"Of course we will," McGuigan said.

"Let me have another look at your identity cards."

He inspected them, glancing from one man to the other several times.

Reluctantly, he turned again. For the second time they watched him climb the stairs, a single flight giving on to a glimpse of landing. As he went from sight, the two detectives glanced at one another. Before either could speak, the old man appeared once more. Leaning over the banister, he peered down at them, then retreated.

"Checking we're not stealing the silver," McGuigan said.

"Pensioners are told to be careful."

"That'll be right."

They waited in silence. Listening, Meldrum could hear a door opening. A moment later, Robertson appeared holding a slip of paper in one hand and a pen in the other.

"Sorry I kept you waiting," he said, handing the paper to Meldrum. "I was as quick as I could be."

"I'm sure you were."

The old man squeezed past them and opened the front door.

"One thing," Meldrum said, "would you have a phone number for her?"

"The only reason I have her address is it was on some document that passed between us. What would I want a phone number for?"

"To contact your daughter?" Meldrum asked.

"She knows my address. You tell me she used it without asking me whether she could. If she ever wanted to speak to me, she'd find me in the phone book."

"If she needed help, you mean," Meldrum said.

When they were outside, McGuigan looked at his companion's face. It was flushed and a vein showed in his forehead.

"What was that about?" the sergeant asked. Getting no answer, he shrugged and said philosophically, "So he's a bastard. Plenty of them about."

CHAPTER
THIRTY-SIX

They kept silent on the way back to Edinburgh, each man busy with his own thoughts. It was late, and they settled on calling on Keeley Robertson's mother the next morning. When he'd dropped the sergeant off, Meldrum took over the driving and was glad to be on his own. On the way down Leith Walk, he pulled in and bought a pie supper with onion rings. He put the heating on in his flat, lifted old newspapers off the chairs and made a pot of coffee, wandering about until the living room felt warm enough to sit in. Three minutes on reheat in the microwave and he emptied the parcel on to a plate and stuffed the crumpled greasy paper into the bin, which he'd forgotten again to empty.

The interview with Keeley Robertson's father had left his mind full of memories of his own daughter, and it was hard for him not to feel that her life might have been better if he had been more there for her. In the slippery fashion of such self-criticism, he found himself going over her childhood and finding something to blame in himself even in the devotion he had given to his job.

Too restless to settle for the night, he felt a strong need to see his daughter and grandson. A phone call brought his ex-wife Carole to the phone and he asked, "Could I speak to Mr Corrigan, please?" Told the husband was out, he promptly clapped the phone down, put on his jacket and went out. Twenty minutes later, he was at the house in Barnton.

When Carole opened the door, he caught her hesitation before letting him inside. Still in the hall, he said, "You look tired. Are you all right?" Feeling protective towards her was a habit he'd never learned to break.

"Was that you on the phone?" And when he didn't answer, "I knew it was. Right in the middle of saying Don was out, I knew."

"I just wanted to see Betty and the wee one."

"Betty's out."

"Can I see Tommy?"

"He's —" Had she been going to say the child was out, too? If so, she was forestalled.

A small voice drifted downstairs. "Gra-a-anny!"

Meldrum made a move towards the stairs, but she caught him by the sleeve. "Stay here!"

"Why?"

"Please. I'll only be a minute."

It would have been easy to take the flight in long strides after her, but his sense of discipline, of what it meant to be law abiding and, perhaps, his pride kept him still until she returned slowly down the stairs and made her way past him into the living room.

"Can I have a seat at least?"

"If you want to."

"I take it that means Corrigan won't be back soon."

As he spoke, he seated himself in one of the plump overstuffed chairs that surrounded the open fireplace. He knew the couple had been at this address for half a dozen years, yet looking round it struck him that the room seemed as fresh and empty of individuality as the furnished room in a showhouse.

"He's out at a dinner."

"Partners not invited?"

"I'm happy to be here to look after Tommy."

She hadn't taken a seat, and he looked up at her where she stood poised as if waiting for him to go.

"I'd like to go up and say goodnight to him."

"He's asleep."

"All right, I'll just look in. Just to see him." He pulled himself up, dismayed by the note of pleading in his voice.

With a sigh, Carole took the seat opposite him. Her hands wound together in her lap.

"He'd see you too. He isn't asleep. He's lying awake."

"Well, then?"

"He'd want to talk to you. The two of you would talk. He'd tell Don."

"Why shouldn't he?"

"There's no point in being angry," she said.

Meldrum became aware of his right fist resting on the chair arm and forced it to unclench.

"Why shouldn't the boy tell Corrigan? I'm his grandfather."

"Don doesn't want you to visit again. He was annoyed after you left."

A surge of protest went through his head, so many objections that one got in the way of another. After a long moment, he had to make do with, "What about you? Don't you have any say in it?"

"Don believes it would be the best thing for Tommy. He's doing it for the boy's sake."

That's shite! Meldrum thought. He said quietly, "How does he make that out?"

She spoke without raising her eyes, watching her hands fold one round the other on her lap. "He felt the boy was upset after you left. What he meant," she looked up at him, "wasn't a criticism. It's because Tommy's fond of you and he needs to get over things and not get upset. Don feels he needs some time to settle down."

Meldrum got up in a single convulsive movement.

"You've forgotten more about children than tha—" he swallowed the word, "will ever know. I've no idea what he's done to brainwash you. Just don't insult me by pretending you believe any of it."

When she didn't answer, he went out into the hall and made his escape.

CHAPTER
THIRTY-SEVEN

In the car the next morning, Meldrum was conscious of a throbbing behind his eyes and a faint nausea. It was unusual for him to have any of the effects of a hangover, not a good thing since it meant there was no penalty to act as a restraint. He'd known men with the same constitution who drank cheerfully until the morning their livers gave up. To be even faintly under the weather meant he must have drunk a lot after leaving Carole the previous night. Carefully he avoided watching the buildings stream past. Fixing his eyes on the dash, he recalled one part of the largely lost hours. At some point, he'd gone to the hotel where the whore Marie plied her trade. He couldn't now be sure why. Had he wanted to take her to bed? If he had, he didn't get the chance, for the waiter whom he and McGuigan had talked to about Michael Thorne had come over to his table and muttered discreetly, "She's not here." Why had the cheeky swine said that? He must have asked the man about her. Bloody fool! Meldrum berated himself. "Not here." He must have asked why the hell not, for he could picture the man's face going sharp and wary as he said, "She came in and I told her to go away. Her face was all marked up. She'd tried to cover the bruises but I couldn't have her in here." With a note of apology, "It wasn't on."

Inwardly, Meldrum groaned at the whole sorry idea that there was now a waiter in the world who thought of him as being in search of an unfortunate for hire who had been shown the door earlier because some bastard had beaten her up. It didn't fit with his image of who he was. He felt as if he had slipped on a steep slope and was vainly clawing his fingers into the mud to halt his downward slide. Once again, the question tormented him, What's happening to me?

"Wonder what the mother will be like," McGuigan said, eyes on the road ahead.

Meldrum glanced across and felt a touch of amusement. McGuigan was a master of protracted silences, but on this occasion without intending to it seemed he had outwaited him.

"Can't be worse than the father," McGuigan said.

Meldrum remembered a joke he'd heard once. He wasn't much of a hand for jokes, but this one had stuck in his memory. An old farmer in a railway carriage asked the other occupant a series of questions intended to make him indicate his destination. Every one brought an evasion, until at last the farmer cried out in rage, *I suppose you think I give a damn where you're going?*

"Soon find out," McGuigan said.

Mrs Robertson lived in a flat not far from Bruntsfield Links. It was a district of old stone tenements, good flats with high corniced ceilings and tiled entries, mostly now fitted with locked street doors

167

and entryphones. In the early Eighties, a four bedroom flat here might have gone for under thirty thousand; now the price could be ten times higher. The buzzer went and Meldrum pushed the door. They climbed until on the third floor they came on the right name on a brass doorplate.

"Have you found her yet?" the mother asked as soon as she saw them.

She was fifty perhaps, a woman who must once have been pretty, and now looked tired with the lines around the eyes of a heavy smoker; still trim though in trousers and a white shirt.

"We're hoping you can help us with that." As they went inside, he went on, "As I said on the phone, the difficulty is that she didn't provide the College with an Edinburgh address."

She turned abruptly, so that he bumped against her. Ignoring his apology, she asked, "What address did she give?"

"Her father's one in North Berwick."

"Do you want tea? It's just made."

She came back into her sitting room bringing a tray with cups, teapot, milk and sugar.

"Milk for both of you? Help yourself to sugar. I nearly forgot to bring it. It's only there for visitors." Bending over the tray, she went on in the same tone, "There's no accounting for what they'll do. She doesn't even like her father. Why not give this address? She stayed with me here until she went off in the middle of her first term. Said she wanted to be in digs. You won't have the comforts you get here, I told her. She could have given this address. I inherited the flat from an aunt. It came at just the right time."

For what? Meldrum wondered, and guessed for the separation from her husband. A lot of couples were held together by their inability to afford two properties.

"Do you know where she stayed in Edinburgh?" Meldrum asked.

"She stayed with friends. One of those student flats. You know, they're all over this district. So many — what do they call them? — multiple occupations."

That didn't sound like the flat owned by Shona Flett in which Colin Halliday lodged; and neither of them would count as "student friends". It began to look as if the girl, a long shot at best, was nothing to do with the case.

The mother must have felt the daughter going off to lodgings implied some criticism of her for she said, "They all do it, you know. We got on perfectly well. She'd have been welcome to stay here. She didn't have to go off into digs."

By a natural reflex, this suggested to Meldrum that the two of them had probably been at odds when the girl left.

"You'll have been in touch regularly," he said.

"Yes. Well. Regularly. What does regularly mean at that age? She wasn't in and out. Too taken up with the course and new friends. You know what they're like at that age."

"When was the last time you heard from her?"

The woman flushed and gave him a look of dislike. "Weeks. Weeks and weeks. I don't know why you wanted to make me say that. What's the point?" She seemed suddenly on the point of tears. "What's the point?" she said again. "It isn't kind."

"We're only trying to make sure she's all right," McGuigan said.

She gave him a look of fright. "That's not what you said when you phoned," she said to Meldrum. "You wanted her help with something. I thought you wanted her as a witness, something like that."

"I don't think I said anything about being a witness," Meldrum said.

"Well, you didn't say anything about her not being all right. Has something happened to her?"

"We've no reason to think so."

"Why are you looking for her then?"

Meldrum fell back on the stock answer. "She might be able to help with our enquiries."

To his surprise, she accepted it. Perhaps she had confronted her own fears and was happy to be deflected from them.

Smiling at him as if he had offered her reassurance, she said, "She's a lovely girl. Not just in looks, though she is a lovely girl that way too. She inherited my mother's red hair. My mother had lovely hair, not that brassy red, but soft with a glow to it. People would look after her in the street. It was just the same with Keeley." She gave them a serious look and as if confiding a secret leaned forward and said quietly, "It was her father who named her Keeley. I never liked the name. In Glasgow — where I come from — it would mean a hooligan. That's what people used to say, you know, oh him, he's just a Glasgow keelie. My husband was furious when I said that. He called it nonsense. He was — is — a difficult — you've met him!"

Meldrum resisted the temptation to nod.

She seemed to catch some sense of his agreement, though, for again her face broke into a smile. When she smiled, she looked ten years younger; ageing again as it faded. "When she left — in the middle of the first term — she gave me an address. I went up there to see her. Not right away, I wasn't being nosey, nothing like that. There was a letter had come for her, anyway I was passing, it seemed silly not to take it up to her. But I was told she'd left there. I was embarrassed. Next time she phoned, I told her how embarrassed I'd been that I didn't know. The girl who told me gave me a funny look, she said Keeley hasn't been here for ages, she was no sooner here than she left, we'd to find someone else. I told Keeley all that and she said they weren't nice and she had to get away. So where are you? I asked her."

Meldrum waited patiently as she stared off into the distance. At last he asked, "She gave you her new address?"

Mrs Robertson slowly shook her head. "She said she'd give me it. But she never did."

CHAPTER
THIRTY-EIGHT

Next morning, instead of getting up at once as he usually did, Meldrum lay staring at the ceiling as he struggled for a firm hold on what had come to him at the drifting moment between one state and the other as he woke up. He didn't want it to dissipate or seem unimportant or a fragment of a dream. Had it been a dream? He went over it again. The night before last in the hotel bar the waiter had said to him that Marie had been asked to leave because her face carried the evidence of a beating. He had no doubt that the conversation had actually taken place even if it meant assuming that first he must have asked the waiter about her, although he had no memory of doing so. The one-sided conversation had come back to him yesterday, what the waiter had said to him, nothing of what he had said to the waiter. Now this morning, just as he wakened, he'd seen the waiter's face and heard him say, "With the other policeman, the one who was with you." What question from him had brought that answer from the waiter? From the look on the man's face (what was it? reluctance? malice? apprehension?) not an innocent one. Could he have asked who Marie had been with before her beating?

It would have been an easy way out to believe it was a dream, one of those put together from bits of the day before like a car welded out of metal and parts from scrapyard wrecks. Easier to believe, but he didn't believe it.

It was a busy frustrating morning. They spoke to staff at the College and no one could give them anything useful about Keeley Robertson. David Lawrence, the maths lecturer, said, "Of course I noticed when she was missing." He smiled. "She was a beautiful girl."

"You noticed that," McGuigan said neutrally.

But Lawrence was fast and bright. "Did someone suggest I was having an affair with her?"

"Why would anyone do that?"

"There was a little bother last year. A girl got pregnant."

Listening to him, Meldrum thought, maybe not so bright after all. He seemed to be doing a good case of hanging himself, which probably meant he was innocent — in this instance of having sex with Keeley Robertson.

From there, they'd gone to have another unsatisfactory interview with Colin Halliday, an interview largely conducted by McGuigan. As far as Meldrum was concerned, there was little point in a fresh interview since they had no new information with which to put pressure on Halliday. As the two talked, he sat back, more conscious of McGuigan than Halliday. At one point, he found himself studying the back of the sergeant's right hand where it rested on his knee. There was no sign of swelling or bruising on the knuckles.

173

At the end of the morning, they were no further forward. Even the students who'd shared the extra classes in maths and religious education with her claimed not to know her well. "I think Sally Farrell is friendlier with her," one of the girls claimed. "But Sally didn't need to do this stuff before term." "It was a surprise when Keeley did," a second said. "She got good grades up till Christmas, but then something must have gone wrong."

They were in the car when McGuigan exclaimed, "Damn! We didn't get a photograph."

As soon as he'd said it, Meldrum knew what he was talking about. The shadow that had been haunting him came back: What's wrong with me? They could have got a photograph of Keeley Robertson from her father. Failing that, there had been the mother. Even this morning, the office at the College might have held one as part of her application. And he knew the first thing they could have done with it: shown it to Colin Halliday's neighbours. If they had recognised the girl as one of the two women who'd hung about the flat, then there would have been ammunition to unleash while interviewing him. Not too late, they'd get a photograph, try the neighbours. But why hadn't it been done? For some reason, he didn't blame McGuigan, perhaps because the sergeant had pointed out the omission. He blamed himself and even went so far as to wonder if McGuigan was mocking him for it.

As these thoughts went through his mind, he noticed McGuigan's left hand on the steering wheel. One of the knuckles was red and puffy. Was McGuigan right or left handed? If he was going to hit someone, which hand would he use?

"Did you see Marie again?" he heard himself asking. The question said aloud shocked him. He'd intended to keep quiet and watch, that was the way to handle suspicion.

"Marie who?"

A smart alec answer. Why not admit it like a man? Meldrum flared with anger he tried not to show.

"The prostitute that old Michael Thorne used."

"See her again? What gave you that idea?"

"She was beaten up the other night."

"But what —" He broke off and Meldrum watched the knuckles of the hand on the wheel whiten.

They sat in silence until they pulled into the car park at St Leonards.

"I think you've gone fucking mad," McGuigan said as he got out of the car and slammed the door.

In the corridor, as Meldrum hurried furiously to catch him up, a young constable stopped him with the news that ACC Fairbairn wanted a word.

CHAPTER
THIRTY-NINE

The Assistant Chief Constable was no friend to Meldrum and the grilling about the investigations into the deaths of Michael Thorne and Shona Flett went on for almost forty minutes. In the face of his superior's smoothly masked hostility, Meldrum was conscious that what he was sketching was less progress than the lack of it. Their talk ended with Fairbairn emphasising that what he'd been told made him even more sceptical about any meaningful connection between the two murders.

As a result, the team was assembled and had been kicking their heels for half an hour by the time Meldrum arrived. Already depressed by having to argue his corner with the unsympathetic Fairbairn, Meldrum found the catch-up meeting hard going. As one unsatisfactory report after another was delivered and no one offered a spontaneous idea or showed a spark of enthusiasm, it came to him that McGuigan, who had contributed almost nothing, was the source from which disaffection radiated to contaminate the whole team. It was urgently necessary to take a grip or the investigation would go sour. This isn't about you, he tried to tell himself, it's about two victims who deserve better than anything we're managing here. He let his gaze travel round them where they sat slouched at desks or leaning against the wall. Too many of them avoided his eye. To his dismay, he could find no energy to unleash on the group. If he couldn't galvanize them, he was in serious trouble. It was a moment of crisis. The silence stretched as they waited for him to speak. What would happen if I picked up a chair and smashed it on that front desk Sharkey is sprawled over? What would happen if I started screaming? What would happen if I started weeping?

Instead, no more than quarter of an hour later, he was in a side room talking to Detective Sergeant Keith Fraser, a balding forty-year-old with the brick complexion of a man who hill walked all the year round. Fraser had been assigned to the murder during the previous night of a tourist. The victim had been found dumped in an alley with impact injuries suggesting that he had been pushed out of a moving vehicle. His half naked corpse lay near a scatter of clothing almost certainly thrown out after him from the same vehicle.

"The way he'd been stabbed," Fraser said, "made me think of that woman Flett. She was mutilated, right? And that took me on to your other case."

"Michael Thorne?"

"Right."

"Fairbairn doesn't believe the two are connected." Meldrum knew how the ACC's mind worked. The last thing he would want would be to create the press feeding frenzy any suggestion of a serial killer would

177

whip up. "No chance he'll want to see a third one tied in as well."

"Aye, but he's going to have to," Fraser said.

"What'll make him do that?"

What was said then took them both across the town centre to the forensic laboratory from which Fraser had just come.

They were expected and were taken through to the room where two hairs were focused into brilliant relief, one laid on a glass slide on the stage of a compound light microscope, the other on a second slide on the stage of a similar instrument. The elements that made up a comparison microscope were completed by an optical bridge, which allowed the two hairs to be viewed simultaneously.

"The one on the left," the technician explained "is from the Thorne case. It's one of the three he had in his fist — we were lucky with it. He pulled it out by the root — under the microscope you can see where it's stretched. Luckily, as I say, some tissue came with it. The one on the right fell out naturally — the root is club-shaped. It was on the jacket of the coat found beside the victim." He straightened up and rubbed his eyes. "The hairs that were pulled out were still growing, that's what we call the anagen phase. The one on the jacket was in the resting or telegen phase. About ten per cent of the hairs on a human head are in that phase — those are the ones that come loose easily, the ones you find in your hairbrush. They can be shed on to the shoulder of a jacket, your own or someone else's, in this case the victim's. No way of telling if it was by primary

178

or secondary transfer — that is whether it came directly from the woman's head to this jacket, primary transfer, or whether it fell from the woman's head on to her clothing and from there to the man's jacket, what we call secondary transfer."

"You can tell that it belongs to a woman?" Fraser asked.

"The one that was torn out certainly does. On its own, the shed hair would be harder to be sure of — even if its length would make it probably female. But although the basic morphology of human hairs is shared throughout the population, the arrangement, distribution and appearance of the characteristics let us differentiate between individuals. These two are from the same individual, which means, yes, both hairs are from a woman."

"I thought you needed a bigger sample," Meldrum said. "I've seen twenty-five hairs from all over the scalp asked for. I could see this being queried if it came to giving evidence in a court."

The technician looked at Fraser to answer this.

Fraser shrugged and said to Meldrum, "I think you should look at them for yourself." To the technician, he said, "Not magnified. Just the way they would be normally."

As the technician stepped aside, Meldrum bent to the eyepiece.

It took only a glance to understand what Fraser had been hinting at. Glowing under the microscope, the two hairs were so striking it was easy to accept that they must have come from the same woman.

As he looked he recalled the missing student Keeley Robertson and could hear a woman's voice whispering to him: "She inherited my mother's red hair. My mother had lovely hair, not that brassy red, but soft with a glow to it. It was just the same with Keeley."

CHAPTER
FORTY

The dead man's name was Nicholas Aaron and he had a brother, who sat now opposite Meldrum with an air of mingled grief and bemusement.

"What was he doing up here? He'd no friends here or relatives. There was no kind of business that might bring him here. He's never been in Scotland, never mind Edinburgh. *I've* never been in Scotland. I don't understand it."

"If he decided to take a break," Meldrum suggested, "why not Edinburgh? It's a popular destination."

"A break? A short holiday? Why now? Anyway, where we live the natural thing would be to hop over the Channel for a weekend. Into the car and through the tunnel. That would be the easiest way." He stared out of the window behind Meldrum's desk. It was one of those September mornings on which a particular shade of grey unbroken cloud settles on the city; a morning made for grief. "I mean he'd go where it was *warm*."

"The Festival's still on. Could he have come for that?"

"What Festival?"

Meldrum explained.

Charles Aaron shook his head decidedly. "Nick wasn't interested in music or plays. He liked a game of golf, a drink with his mates. He took his wife to the pictures sometimes, but that would be it. And out to restaurants, he enjoyed a good meal out."

Accepting that when it came to food France might have the edge, Meldrum offered, "There is a Film Festival just now as well." The main festival, a book festival, a film festival; hadn't there been a jazz festival, too, at one time? He'd a vague idea that the film festival came at the beginning of the three weeks. If so, it would be over. And wasn't this the last weekend of the Festival proper? He wasn't sure.

Again, Charles Aaron gave a decisive negative. "Film festival? Foreign films, you mean? Nick never went near those kinds of cinemas." His tone made Meldrum think of the grubby venues dived into by men in dirty raincoats once upon a time. Now they'd stay home and get what they wanted on TV or the computer. At the idea of computers, he felt the shadow of a possibility stirring. For the moment, though, he stuck to getting as much out of Aaron as he could. He'd already learned that Charles, a stout swarthy-faced man with dark shiny jowls, at almost fifty, was the older brother. Nick had been in his early forties. The brothers had run a veterinary practice together, and lived within half a mile of each other.

"No money worries?" Meldrum asked.

"Making money hand over fist. Sarah might want to sell up, of course, take her share out of it."

"Your brother's wife?"

"Never know what she'll do."

"Did she and your brother get on?"

"What does that mean?"

"Was it a good marriage?"

"That's a hell of a question at a time like this."

"You said yourself, he had to have a reason to come here. You don't think he was here on holiday, or on business. He wasn't running away from money worries."

"A woman?"

"As a possibility, how does that strike you?"

"I'm not a fool," Aaron said. And, as Meldrum looked puzzled, he wiped the tips of his fingers across his eyes as if suppressing tears. "I'm not foolish enough to think my brother was a saint. But he had a wife and child. I always thought they were happy enough." He looked at Meldrum resentfully. "I know you can't tell about a marriage — not unless you're inside it. But all the same . . . There was never any talk of a woman. A receptionist left, but — hysterical bitch —" He straightened up as if pulling himself together. "He's never been in Edinburgh! Not in his whole life! Where would he have met a woman living up here?"

"On the internet?" Meldrum wondered.

For a moment, the man opposite stared blankly, but then as his expression altered and he glanced away, Meldrum understood that, yes, as far as Nick Aaron's brother was concerned, it was a possibility.

CHAPTER
FORTY-ONE

Once they'd gone through the usual bureaucratic hoops the hard drive of Nicholas Aaron's computer should be sent up by special delivery, but time being of the essence Meldrum asked if meantime someone could look at what it contained. If there was any evidence as to what had brought the victim to Edinburgh, he needed to know it as quickly as possible.

"I've a name for you," the detective constable said. "There are dozens of emails between them and he saved them all."

The woman's name was Babs Hedderwicke.

"Do you have an address for her?"

"Sorry."

"You're sure?"

"I speed read the stuff, but yes I'm sure."

"Give me a second." Meldrum laid the phone down and took the slip of paper with the name on it into the inquiry room. "Try and find an address for this. First name will be Barbara, I suppose. It isn't a common surname."

On the same principle of trying to get information as quickly as possible, he spent another quarter of an hour talking to the DC. "How long had they been in contact?"

"I'm assuming he started saving the emails into a file almost from the off. If so they've been writing back and forward for a bit more than eighteen months. The first couple suggest to me that they first met in a chat room, but I don't know how long it was after meeting that they started on the emails. After a bit, the letters tail off and I'd guess the two of them were using messenger and talking real time. From then, the letters are filling the gaps — going over what they'd said on messenger or talking about things that happened during the day or even stuff on the news, it's as if they couldn't get enough of one another. His letters are written late at night — maybe he waited till the missus had gone to bed."

"You spoke to the wife?"

"No. I wasn't at the house. But from what I'm told, she knew nothing about Babs Hedderwicke. He told her he was going away for a few days to play golf with friends. Next thing she knew she'd us at the door telling her he was dead. She's shattered apparently. Well, no surprise there, I suppose." When Meldrum didn't answer at once, he went on, "And they've a kid. Makes you wonder what the hell these guys think they're playing at."

"Does she describe herself in any of the emails?"

"I took a note. Here we are. Twenty-nine years old. Five six. Brown hair worn long. Brown eyes. 34C." He chuckled. "Uh — she's shaved. Not sure how you'd

185

check that." Met by silence, he hurried on, "Married at nineteen. Separated. No children."

"Brown hair?"

"Worn long."

Too much to hope for that it might have been red. People didn't always tell the truth on the internet, of course.

"One more thing. Did she say what she worked at?"

"Claims to be a lawyer. Couple of things she came up with, though, made me wonder." He chuckled again. "If she was telling porkies, though, you'd think she'd have given herself bigger boobs."

And if a woman had red hair, the kind a man might turn to look after in the street, why would she lie about it?

CHAPTER
FORTY-TWO

They had an argument about whether Grania should walk down to the village.

"We were told to stay here," Emer said. She was sitting on the couch with her legs curled under her. They had started to wear their coats in the house, because of the cold. She could still hear the man's voice as he had come into the house behind her. *God almighty, it's freezing in here!* he'd said, and then he'd groaned as Cadoc stepped out from behind the door and clubbed him on the head. When she'd looked round he was lying on the floor and blood was running from his ear. *At least he won't feel the cold*, the Convenor said coming in from the kitchen. She hadn't known that he, too, was going to be there.

"The Convenor told us to stay here until they came back," Emer said.

"When will that be?"

"Soon."

"Today?"

"Perhaps not today."

"We're out of food. Cadoc brought hardly any. Will dying of hunger help anyone?"

"We won't die."

"You could come with me. There's a limit to what I can carry myself. Even by car it seemed a long time between us passing the edge of the village and getting here. And coming back it will be uphill all the way."

"What if there is no shop in the village?"

"Then I'll walk till I find one where there is a shop. Will you come?"

Stubbornly, Emer had shaken her head, crouching down into the corner of the couch. At that, Grania had swung round and gone by herself. Emer thought, She's strong, she'll manage. And then her thoughts ran together in a kind of endless hallucination of fear and despair and physical suffering.

Even when it was dark, she didn't light one of the candles. There were lamps but they hadn't found any gas containers to put into them. Time became meaningless to her, and when the door opened and Grania came in with a shopping bag in each hand it was as if she had been gone for only a moment. With a soft moan, she dropped the two bags on the floor. "I had to take out the cans of soup," she said. "Otherwise I'd never have made it back. They're lying under a hedge just before you come to where the trees have been burned. We can look for them tomorrow."

Emer sat and watched, moving only her eyes, as Grania lit the candles and took a newspaper out of one of the bags and crumpled the pages and piled them in the grate and laid bits of broken stick on top and lit the twists of paper with matches from a box she took from the other bag. Emer crept from the couch and crouched beside the hearth, so that it was she who saw a face and snatched one of the sheets from on top of the pile.

"It's him," she said, meaning the man they had killed.

She spread the sheet out on the floor and pressed it flat using both hands. It was the front page of the morning paper. Along one edge there was a brown smudge where the flame had come close. DEAD TOURIST IDENTIFIED. She stared at his name under the picture.

"Nicholas Aaron. That can't be right."

"Why not? Didn't you say that was the name he gave you?" Grania asked absently. Rummaging through the bags, she was intent on her task.

"I thought he was giving a false name."

"So he wasn't, what does it matter?"

"Don't you see? It isn't a Lebanese name. It isn't a Muslim name. The Convenor told me he was from the Lebanon."

"Well then he must have been, and he must have given you a false name. What's difficult about that?"

As Emer rubbed her hands over the page, she spread spots of soot into smears that obscured some of the words so that she had to bend close, long red hair brushing the floor.

"It says he has a brother. There's a small photograph of him. 'Charles Aaron, brother of the dead man.' How can it be a false name if he has a brother?" She sat up on her haunches and cried, "I don't understand!"

Grania stood up. She had a loaf in one hand and a box of Flora margarine and block of cheese in the other. "Let's eat," she said.

Later as they sat in the kitchen, Emer said, "Thing is, he made me unsure."

"Who did?"

"Aaron, if that was his name. We talked all the way out in the car. He told me about being a vet, and that he liked working with small animals like cats and dogs. None of that James Herriot stuff, he said. He was so convincing that I wondered if there could have been some mistake. I told myself when we get to the house, I'll see — maybe it's a mistake, I couldn't help thinking." She paused miserably. "But, of course, once we got here, there wasn't time."

She saw the man sprawled on the floor and noticed again the bright thread of blood leaking from his ear.

CHAPTER
FORTY-THREE

"I'm glad you found me," Babs Hedderwicke said.

It was a small flat in a 1920s building in a side street off Morningside Road. As she took them inside, she put her head round the first door in the corridor and said, "It's all right, Mummy. I'll bring you tea in a little while."

As they followed her along the corridor, Meldrum took in the layout — brief glimpse of a front room, sunlight on a yellow carpet, kitchen door open to show a sink and overhead cupboards, a bathroom door with frosted glass and a modesty curtain. Is she taking us into her bedroom? he wondered.

The last door was the one she opened. Not a bedroom. Did she sleep in the same room as her mother? With three of them, the room seemed to be crammed full. A wall unit held manuals and books. A shelf under it with a computer and printer. One computer chair and an easy chair completed the furniture.

"You won't have to say anything to Mummy?" she asked.

"I'd hope not," Meldrum said, "but I can't make any promises."

"No, of course not. I shouldn't have asked."

She was a woman of about fifty with heavy features and lines of weariness cut deeply around the eyes. Not unpleasant looking, just tired and from the looks of things without much in her life, dressed sensibly in heavy shoes and a cardigan over a green blouse tucked into a skirt that came to mid calf. She wore one ring, a ringletted head of a woman mounted on porcelain in a silver setting, and a gold chain round her neck.

"I'm sorry there aren't enough seats," she said. "But Mummy never comes into this room. I put a bolt on the door, but I don't need to use it now. I would have come to you, I think I would. It's just that I was so ashamed. I didn't want people to despise me."

"You may as well sit down," McGuigan said abruptly. "Standing doesn't bother us."

What is he trying to prove? Meldrum thought sourly. That he's too nice to beat up a prostitute?

With a sigh, Babs Hedderwicke sank into the computer chair. The machine Meldrum noted had its stand-by light on, though the screen had gone dark.

Seeing the direction of his glance, she swung round and rubbed the mouse back and forward until the screen lightened and a game of solitaire appeared.

"I keep it on all the time," she said. "It's company for me."

"We'll have to take it," Meldrum said, "to be examined. If it isn't needed in evidence, you should get it back quickly."

"God help me," she said, as if stating a fact. "Do you know all about it?"

"Nicholas Aaron's computer is in police custody," Meldrum said. "He kept all the emails you sent and copies of his to you."

"You've read them?"

"Not yet, but we've been told what they contain."

"You will read them?"

Meldrum nodded.

"Do you have to?" And when he didn't answer, she said, "Of course you do. I don't know how I'll bear it."

"I'm sure if you were fond of Mr Aaron, you'll want us to find who killed him."

"Fond of him? I thought I loved him. Please don't laugh at me."

Meldrum glanced sharply at McGuigan, who gave no sign of wanting to smile, but frowned as he caught the older man looking at him.

"Would you confirm some things for me?" Meldrum asked. "Are we right in thinking that you encountered Mr Aaron in an internet chat room? And then corresponded with him by e-mail?"

"And then we used messenger — it was like talking to him. Late at night when Mummy was asleep. He kept asking me if he could phone and I made excuses. He got angry with me and accused me of being married."

"He was married, did you know that?"

"I'm not a complete fool," she said, with the faintest air of triumph. "He wasn't happy."

"Did you know he had children?" McGuigan asked.

"Oh, dear." After a moment, she said again, "Oh, dear."

Just the one, Meldrum thought, and then decided that made no difference.

He said, "Who suggested meeting?"

Her lips stretched in a horrible parody of a smile. "Do you imagine it was me?"

"He wanted to meet?"

"He kept on about it. I made all kinds of excuses, but it just made him keener. By that time, we knew one another's first names. But then something happened — my whole name appeared in an email, somewhere at the top. I don't know how that happened. And not long afterwards he wrote that he had traced my home address." She gave the same painful smile. "You can do anything with a computer, he told me. He was going to come to Edinburgh. 'I'll hurry from the train straight to your house,' he said."

"Did he threaten you?" McGuigan asked.

"No! It wasn't like that. He'd fallen in love with the woman he thought I was. The woman who made jokes and talked about books and politics. She was twenty-nine, you know."

Meldrum couldn't prevent himself from remembering the rest of the description given by the DC over the phone, but kept his expression carefully blank.

"Did he come to your house?" he asked, and for a moment as she hesitated he had the wild thought that he might be about to hear a confession of murder.

At last she said, "I must make Mummy her tea. I'll only be a moment."

When she'd gone, McGuigan said, "Maybe she's going to do a runner."

194

As he spoke, he smiled as if disclaiming the suggestion. It showed, though, that he'd shared that moment of wondering about a confession.

Time dragged until she returned, but then she'd had to make tea and let it infuse and take it to her mother, plump up her pillows too, probably.

When she came back, she had a tray with the teapot and three cups and a milk jug and sugar bowl.

"Are you allowed to have this?"

"It doesn't count as drinking on duty," McGuigan said, and surprised Meldrum by laughing.

"Milk and sugar?"

"Just as it comes," McGuigan said, sounding more cheerful than Meldrum had heard him for a long time.

She served them both, tea with milk and sugar for Meldrum, black for McGuigan.

Meldrum sipped and asked, looking at her over the cup, "Did he come here?"

"I couldn't let him do that. I told him I was married and that my husband was jealous. I was that desperate. But he still wanted to come to Edinburgh. And that's when I suggested meeting in the Neptune Hotel. We arranged a time, and I was there early. It was madness, of course. I even thought that I might actually talk to him. I had some idea if I spoke to him a miracle might happen. He might see me as the girl in the emails. The bar was almost empty when I arrived. Nowhere to hide I thought. It felt as if the decision had been taken out of my hands. As I sat, I couldn't help imagining that he might get a room and we could spend the night together. I know you're going to ask what about my mother? How would she manage on her own? Would you believe I pushed that thought out of my head? I sat there and I didn't give Mummy a thought. And then he came. He came in at exactly the time he'd said he would come. You see he wasn't playing games with me. He came at the exact time to the minute. I knew then he was someone you could trust with your life."

She sat silent. To get her talking again, Meldrum asked, "Had he sent you a photograph?"

"I recognised him. There wasn't any doubt. When he came in, there were only half a dozen people in the bar. I might have been the only woman. And he looked round and his eye passed over me and he went over to the bar and got a drink and took it to a table and sat waiting. He was waiting for me to come." Drinking from the cup, she used both hands to carry it to her mouth. "There was no way I could introduce myself. It was so ridiculous. I was so ridiculous. I wanted to leave, get as far away from there as I could. But then I realised, what would happen when he knew I wasn't going to come? Maybe he'll go away again, I thought, get on a train and go back where he came from. I knew he would be angry, but if I wrote to him, I could say I'd been ill, and we could go on as we had been. I am so ridiculous. Why would he go without trying to see me, after coming so far? He would go to my flat. I couldn't let him do that."

"What did you do?" Meldrum asked.

"Something happened I could never have expected. This man and woman sat at a table near me. She was facing me, the man had his back to me, but he said something and she looked over her shoulder quickly. The bar was busier by then, but I knew who she was looking at. I thought, oh God, it's someone who knows him. But the man got up and left — and he passed right by Nicholas's table and didn't say a word. I was relieved, and then the girl moved to the other side of the table to the seat he'd been in. That meant she had her back to me, but I knew who she had her eye on. It didn't take long. Nicholas came over and sat down and not long after that, they left together."

"You're telling us this girl knew Nicholas Aaron," McGuigan asked sceptically. His glance at Meldrum said more plainly than words *if she exists.*

"No! I'm sure she didn't. I think the man told her to attract him. And she was so beautiful. Nicholas went with her, I was angry with him. But I can see now, a girl like that, any man would have been tempted."

"Could you describe her?"

"She had the most extraordinary red hair."

Meldrum felt his own hair stir on the back of his neck.

"I'd like you to talk to our people," he said. "They can help you remember her face."

"What about the man?" McGuigan asked.

"No." She made a gesture to show how impossible that would be. "He had his back to me the whole time. He was tall and powerful — I could tell that. And he had black hair. But I didn't see his face."

"If we can find the girl," Meldrum said, "we'll find him."

"Do you think you will?"

"Yes," Meldrum said trying to sound more confident than he felt.

"It's just that I'm certain they didn't know Nicholas. I think they picked him out just because he was in the bar that night. I'm sure that was the only reason. It could have been him or anyone." Her face trembled with a spasm of grief and something like horror. "If he died because of me, how can I live with that?"

CHAPTER
FORTY-FOUR

Nothing like a new murder to freshen up the troops. Not a fair thought, but then, on the other hand, Meldrum decided, why the hell should he be fair?

"I'll tell you what should worry you," he told the assembled detectives. "Babs Hedderwicke was sure that neither the man nor the woman she saw knew Nicholas Aaron. If she's right, they chose their victim at random. They had no reason to pick him rather than anyone else."

"It was the woman who went off with him," McGuigan said.

And your point is? Meldrum thought and went on as if he hadn't heard the interruption. "Aaron was just in the wrong place at the wrong time. But we know the red hairs from his death and Michael Thorne's are a match; and Thorne and Shona Flett are tied by their both being connected to Colin Halliday. A random murder linked to two others sounds like a serial killer. If it is, there's no reason why we might not have a fourth murder or a fifth or sixth or seventh or as many as it takes until we catch him."

"Him?" McGuigan said sharply. "But we know that it isn't just a man on his own." His tone was inappropriate, holding a suggestion of: what the hell are you talking about?

Meldrum looked at him for a lingering moment. Although long practice kept his face without expression, he knew that, even if the tone was wrong, the question was valid. What the hell had made him talk about a single killer? He remembered a precept from Billy Ord, his first and best boss. Never explain, never apologise.

"You're telling us something we don't know?" he asked with a pleasant neutrality, the kind that was felt as contempt but made a man look like a fool if he took offence. "Did you think I'd forgotten the red-headed girl? It looks as if she acted as the bait for Aaron. If so, then it's not impossible she did the same for Michael Thorne. But that doesn't mean she was the one who killed them. From Miss Hedderwicke's description of what happened in the hotel — the man was the one who picked the victim."

"Are we not jumping the gun here?" McGuigan asked. "We know Aaron had the girl's hair on his jacket. But we know anyway that he went off with her. They had some contact, must have had, how otherwise would her hair have got on his jacket? But suppose after that they split up? Maybe quarrelled, maybe she didn't want to have sex. He goes off on his own, meets someone else, and that someone else kills him."

Looking round, Meldrum could see the sergeant had lost his audience with that suggestion. No one fancied the idea of starting from scratch on a murderer who'd appeared out of nowhere later that night.

"You're absolutely right," Meldrum said. "We'll keep an open mind. But it makes sense to work on what we've got." He looked over at John Melrose, a Borderer, who among his other skills was gifted at coaxing e-fit reconstructions out of witnesses. "Meantime, John's been working with Miss Hedderwicke, trying to get some kind of picture of the red-headed girl out of her. How did it go?"

Melrose's long jawed face stretched into an even more lugubrious expression than usual. "Pure bloody hopeless. I don't think the bloody woman used her eyes on the girl at all. For one thing, she was fixated on Aaron. Breaking her heart over him. And that meant, she didn't see the girl as she was, no, what she was seeing was somebody so bloody wonderful that any man would prefer her. The red hair was, I quote, 'like a film star'. But she was so busy being knocked out by the hair and feeling like shit about herself that the girl's face was just a blur. And that's what I've got. I honestly think it would be a waste of time to try it on anybody."

"Great," Meldrum said heavily.

"We've always got the photo of Keeley Robertson," McGuigan said. "We finally got one from the College. We could try it on the Hedderwicke woman."

"Keeley Robertson's not under suspicion of anything," Meldrum said. "All she's done is disappeared. She turns up and finds we've been showing her photo as someone who's gone off with a guy who got himself murdered . . .? All she'd need would be a good lawyer."

201

"But we showed it to Colin Halliday's neighbours," McGuigan protested, "even if the dozy bastards made nothing of it."

"Not the same thing," Meldrum said. "We were just looking for a missing tenant as far as they were concerned. And, as you say, they were useless. Red hair, yes, face not a chance."

It was Sharkey the joker who unexpectedly summed it up. "The bugger of it is the Shona Flett killing. The red hairs match for Thorne and Aaron. We know Thorne used prostitutes and Aaron sounds the type as well. It all fits for those two. But Shona Flett? It doesn't make sense!"

CHAPTER
FORTY-FIVE

Having decided it was time to talk again to Colin Halliday, Meldrum found it frustrating when a phone call yielded the information that he hadn't been into College for a few days.

"A week's work would kill these people," McGuigan grumbled.

Neither man's mood was improved when no one seemed to be at home in the Marchmont flat.

"He's not there," Meldrum said.

"Either that or the bugger's hiding," McGuigan said, refusing to take his thumb from the bellpush.

Meldrum turned away and started at a run down the stairs, taking them three at a time, passing a woman coming up.

"Hold it!" McGuigan said, catching up as Meldrum was about to emerge into the street.

Meldrum felt a flush of pure rage. "What?"

"Didn't you see her?"

"See who?" See fucking who?

But even as he asked, he saw her coming down the stairs toward them. Small, neat, black haired, about sixty perhaps. The woman he'd passed.

"Mrs Halliday," he said. "Going to visit your son? Looks like he isn't in."

Her eyes flickered from one to the other. No question but that she knew who they were.

"You're looking for Colin?"

"We wanted to talk to him."

She smiled a shade uncertainly, looking less confident than the first time they had spoken to her. "If you see him," she said, "please don't mention I was coming up to see him."

"Why would that be?" McGuigan asked.

"He prefers to come to see me."

"He doesn't want you to visit him?"

She gave the same tentative smile. "He likes to have his own life. Young people are like that."

"Have you ever been in his flat?" McGuigan asked.

"Of course!"

"Would you mind telling me how often you've been in it?" McGuigan persisted.

"What an extraordinary thing to ask!"

"It's just that last time we spoke you gave the impression that you and your son had been very close since your husband left."

"We have been."

"But maybe you don't see all that much of him?"

A small rain was sleeting down and drifting in on them as they stood just inside the mouth of the close.

"There's a café across the road," Meldrum said. "Would you like a coffee? We could talk in there."

From where he was standing, he could see that the place was empty, half a dozen tables islanded forlornly in the dim afternoon light.

When they were settled and the tea had been brought by a stout girl who took herself off again into the back shop, Meldrum asked, "Did you enjoy your holiday?"

"Very nice. My ex-husband bought the flat there. It came to me as part of the settlement. Being able to get away to the sun can save your sanity in this climate."

"Weather's been all right," McGuigan said, "off and on."

"Still, nice to get away. And there was nothing to keep me."

They drank tea in silence while they thought about that.

As Meldrum opened his mouth, she asked, "Are you any nearer finding who killed Michael?"

"Have you seen your son since you got back from holiday?" A question for a question, an old technique.

"I phoned him all yesterday afternoon, but didn't get him in. That's why I came down. Has something happened?"

Meldrum stirred the spoon in his cup as he made up his mind what to say. "Were you in touch with him while you were away?"

"No. But we don't usually phone when I'm in Spain. I don't even send a postcard." She gave a brief smile, which faded at once.

"Nothing's happened to your son. His landlady was murdered."

"But that's awful. Poor woman. Where did it happen?"

"She was found on a beach near North Berwick. Her name was Shona Flett. Did you ever meet her?"

"Why on earth would I have met Colin's landlady?"

"She lived in the flat."

"With Colin?"

Meldrum nodded.

"I don't mean *with*," she said. "I didn't mean that the way it sounded. There must have been other tenants. You know what the flats round here are like."

"Full of students," McGuigan said, making it sound like a perversity.

"Were there? Other tenants, that is?"

"The truth is we don't know. Your son says not."

"Well, that must be right. He tells the truth." And with a touch of the lateral thinking that had marked their first interview with her, added emphatically, "He teaches religious studies, you know."

While Meldrum was finding no immediate answer to that, McGuigan eased a photograph from the inside pocket of his jacket.

"Have you ever seen this woman?"

As he angled it towards her, Meldrum saw that it was a copy of the photograph they had obtained from the College.

"What lovely hair. I wonder if it looks like that in real life. Who is she?"

Watching her, Meldrum couldn't be sure. Had something altered in her expression as she looked at the photograph?

"Her name is Keeley Robertson," McGuigan said. "Did you ever hear your son mention that name?"

"Keeley Robertson? Keeley — is that one of these modern names? No, I'm sure my son never mentioned her. Why on earth should he?"

"She was one of his students."

Mrs Halliday looked at McGuigan with a kind of fright. "Did something happen to her, too?"

"Not as far as we know."

"Well then?" She turned a baffled look on Meldrum.

Forced to take part, he said, "She seems to have disappeared."

"Are you searching for her?"

"It's not quite so certain as that. Lots of young people go off in the summer. It's just that she had classes this month and hasn't been there."

"I don't understand," she said.

"If your son gets in touch," Meldrum said, "tell him we need to talk to him."

McGuigan picked up the photograph from the table where she had laid it. "You're sure you've never heard the name or seen her?"

"What was —"

"Keeley Robertson." Something in his tone made Meldrum wonder if he too had caught her hesitation when shown the girl's photograph.

She shook her head. Looking at Meldrum, she said, "You didn't answer me when I asked about Michael's murder."

"We won't stop searching."

She sighed. "It seems like another life. We weren't unhappy together. He wasn't a bad man."

There was nothing to say to that. Not a bad man, Meldrum thought, that would look all right on a tombstone.

Pushing his cup back, he was about to get to his feet, when she said with a jerk of the head as if shaking water from her hair, "I blame that woman."

"Bridget O'Neill," McGuigan offered. If he had a weakness, Meldrum had observed, it was his need to impress with the quickness of his understanding.

"Bridget O'Neill. He fathered a child on her and he never married her. And him a Catholic. That must tell you something."

"You knew about the child?"

"And that he'd been a Catholic?" McGuigan added.

"Just before he walked out on me and *my* child, he told me about being a priest and the woman he'd fallen in love with. To hear him tell it, until he met her he'd never looked at a woman 'carnally'. That's what he called it. *Carnally*." She drew out the word, drawling it parodically. "God almighty, by that time he must have been in his twenties! What do they do to those boys? Some of them will be gay, of course. But he wasn't. I could sign a certificate to that. Would you believe he was in tears? And that I felt sorry for him? Women are fools. Next thing he was gone. Can you imagine how I felt trying to explain to the congregation of the Pentecostal Church that their charismatic minister had decamped?" She started to laugh. To Meldrum's surprise it sounded genuine. A remarkable woman, he thought, Thorne was probably a fool to have left her. But then, if women were fools, men were worse. "I didn't know where he'd gone. But I came back to Edinburgh — why not, my mother was still alive then. I didn't know he was here. All these years, I might have been walking along and met him. That would have been a shock. What would we have said to one another?"

"You never did meet him?"

"No."

"Your son Colin, did he ever try to find his real father?"

"Why do you ask that?"

"Children sometimes do."

"I suppose," she said. "In my experience, girls more than boys." Perhaps changing the subject, she said, "Maybe I should have guessed he might be up here. This woman Bridget lived in a cottage just outside Edinburgh. At least, that's what he told me that last night. Confessing to me, a priest's habit, I suppose. He told me he'd met her when he went to Edinburgh for a conference about God in the modern world. Isn't life a farce?"

But Meldrum was leaning forward. He felt McGuigan watching him, alerted. It was as if his blood ran faster in his veins.

Quietly, almost casually, he asked, "A cottage outside Edinburgh? Was that all? He didn't mention where?"

"It was a long time ago. Does it matter?"

"No," Meldrum said. "I don't suppose it does."

"I've put Michael out of my mind all these years. But when you showed me that photograph, I remembered him telling me his Bridget had this wonderful red hair. I should have hated him, but I cried when I learned how he died alone."

CHAPTER
FORTY-SIX

From the flat stretch of rough moor just under the summit, the two men looked down on sheep drifting across the flank of the hill and far below that to fields of pasture on the far side of a ribbon of road and red rooftops among the trees marking the half curve of a small town in the distance.

"What else could I do?" Cadoc asked.

"What you were told?"

"I was desperate. I knew it was only a matter of time before those two policemen came back."

"So you decided it would look better if you weren't there."

"I was running out of lies to tell."

"But you don't tell lies. You work out what the truth should be for them and stick to that."

"I just needed to get away."

"Without discipline there isn't any safety."

"Is all the killing over?"

The Convenor took a deep breath. "Up here," he said, "it feels as if you could live forever. Do you share that illusion?"

The wind was from the northeast and Cadoc felt it chilling the bones of his face. What would it be like in these hills in the winter, he wondered? How would the two women and he survive in that bare house?

He realised that the Convenor had started off again, not waiting for a response. He began to hurry after him, and found himself having to break into a trot to try to catch up with the older man's stride that made nothing of the broken ground. Once he'd come up with him, the pace was still set at a rate which made him uncertain of his footing so that he had to concentrate on every step. His breath caught in his chest as they sped down the steep slope to the track that would take them back to the house where the women waited.

"I want you to come back with me," the Convenor said.

"In your car?"

"Don't be stupid."

"You want me to follow you back into town?"

"Back to the flat. I've got someone coming in to look at it tomorrow night. Stay overnight. Go to work tomorrow. Show them round the flat when they come."

"Someone wanting to buy it?"

"Someone has to."

"Will you be there?"

"I'll tell you what to say."

"And then can I come back out to the house?"

"I'll tell you when. You shouldn't be in too much of a hurry to come back."

There must have been something in his tone for Cadoc stopped as if a hand had been placed on his chest.

"Why not? You said that we wouldn't be safe in Edinburgh. And won't it be worse now that we've killed another of them?"

The Convenor had gone on two or three long paces. He stopped and Cadoc stared at the broad column of his back, wondering if he meant to look round or just walk away from him. When he did turn, it was a relief that he didn't seem angered. There was even a little twitch of the lips, almost a smile as he said, "Think about it. If it gets so bad that you can't keep your old life, what would that mean? And not just for you? For all three of you."

It was said so reasonably and with such a lack of emotion that Cadoc was made to understand as if it had been spelled out to a child that they had no future, not in the house below, not in Edinburgh, not anywhere.

CHAPTER
FORTY-SEVEN

Babs Hedderwicke was reluctant since her already low confidence had been damaged by DC Melrose's failure entirely to conceal his scorn at her efforts to help him make some kind of e-fit of the woman she had seen going off from the hotel bar with Nicholas Aaron. It took some effort by McGuigan to persuade her before she brought Keeley Robertson's photograph up almost to her nose and held it for what seemed an endless moment. But when she lowered it, her eyes were wide with excitement. "That's her!" she cried.

McGuigan couldn't restrain a glance of triumph. He'd had to argue with Meldrum to show the photograph, pushing against a weakness in the DI, which he'd never felt before. Even now, he was too canny to put this new perception into words to anyone else, contenting himself with sniping and sly asides. The truth, one its victim too was trying to conceal, from himself above all, was that Meldrum was battling a constant feeling that none of it mattered, that nothing mattered, a feeling of indifference.

Even as McGuigan showed his sense of being justified, Meldrum knew that it was a very qualified victory. The chances were low of it ever being used in a court; any good lawyer would tie the woman Hedderwicke in knots; and the likeliest outcome would be some kind of reprimand for the policemen involved — with him taking most of the blame.

As all this went through his mind, he heard Babs Hedderwicke say again, with something of the note of a child who had managed to please the adults, "It's her!" A claim which she followed at once with the intended confirmation, "That lovely hair! And I recognise the blue jacket!"

Blue? Meldrum thought.

It was his turn to glance at McGuigan, in time to see the awful possibility dawn on the sergeant. Even a mediocre defence counsel would manage to deal with a witness suffering from green-blue colour blindness.

A lesser man might have been tempted to allow himself a shake of the head. Meldrum concentrated on being courteous to the woman and getting them out of her house in as good order as possible.

Once outside, too, it was he who made the point, "It's still an identification. She'd be a liability in court, but it doesn't mean she is wrong. And if it was Keeley Robertson who lured Nicholas Aaron out of the hotel, then she is also the woman who was with Michael Thorne the night he died."

"And she's Colin Halliday's student."

"And she's Colin Halliday's student," Meldrum agreed.

"Question is, where the hell is she?"

"Come to that, where's Colin Halliday?"

CHAPTER
FORTY-EIGHT

The house seemed even darker than before. As he sat down, Meldrum saw spots of yellow against the shadows.

"I didn't expect you back," Antony Crowe said, adding, "so soon." He smiled as if he'd intended some sort of joke. "What can I do for you?"

"We're looking for Colin Halliday."

"I wouldn't have known who you were talking about a month ago."

"That right?" McGuigan asked. "Your friend Shona Flett never mentioned him? She was his flatmate."

"To be precise, his landlady," Crowe said. "And now I'm his landlord."

"We've tried him at the flat more than once," Meldrum said. "He wasn't there. The neighbours haven't seen him the last few days."

"But why should I know where he is?"

"Have you given him notice yet?"

"Not yet."

"So he's still living in the flat?"

"I assume so."

"What about the rent?" McGuigan asked. "When is it due?"

Crowe threw back his head and laughed. He had one of those rich laughs that made his shoulders shake before settling into a series of quiet chuckles. "Sorry," he said. "But the double act is a bit much. I should know when his rent is due. But I don't. To be honest, I don't even care. After all, the flat to me is like a gift. An unexpected windfall. Why should I chase him for a fortnight's rent, when I'll sell it for thousands of pounds?"

"Some people would," McGuigan said sourly.

"Anyway," Crowe said, getting to his feet, "I hope you find him. Wouldn't the easiest thing be to ask at his work?"

Neither detective volunteered that they had or that Halliday had been missing classes without phoning in an explanation.

As McGuigan also stood up, Meldrum had one of those recalcitrant impulses that had got him in trouble over the years and, just sometimes, given an unpredictable result.

He leaned back in the chair and asked, "Could we have a word with your mother?"

It was McGuigan who turned his head sharply in surprise.

By contrast, Crowe seemed unperturbed, though the dimness of the light might have helped by veiling his expression.

"I'll get her," he said.

After he left the room, McGuigan said quietly, "He didn't ask why."

"Maybe he thinks it's about his alibi."

"Isn't it?" And before Meldrum could answer him, he went in one long pace to the wall and switched on the overhead light. The shadows retreated. "That's better."

When Crowe came in, shepherding his mother in front of him, he blinked once as he took in the brightness. The old lady looked at the two detectives and made her way to the chair by the fireplace. In the improved light, the image above the mantlepiece came into sharp focus. Jesus, head bowed, gazed down on them, his heart red and vivid in his open chest.

"My mother's eyes are sensitive," Crowe said.

"Do you want the light off?" McGuigan directed his question at the mother.

"No, no," Crowe said. "If it's easier for you, she'll manage."

In the hard illumination of a three bulb fixture in the centre of the ceiling, Meldrum, a big man himself, took the measure of Antony Crowe as if seeing him for the first time. Dark thick hair that probably ran in a pelt down his back. With a neck that thick, the shirt would have to be made for him. Broken nose, good looking though. Why was it you could always tell when someone was intelligent? In this case, probably well above the average. When he met Crowe's eyes, they were amused as if he had been listening to the detective's inner commentary.

"You wanted to speak to me?" the mother said.

Meldrum was conscious that all three pairs of eyes had been turned on him.

"When you spoke to us before," Meldrum said, "your son introduced you only as his mother."

"I am his mother."

"Would you mind telling us your full name, please?"

Puzzled by the request, she didn't answer at once. Meldrum took the opportunity to study her in that brief interval. If he was right, she was only in her mid-sixties, not old by today's standards. Could she have been ill? Her face was heavily lined, with deep scores cut around the upper lip of a mouth that had folded in on itself. The eyes, too, were heavy lidded with the kind of swollen pouches under them that suggested water retention, a condition which might have a number of causes, including heavy drinking. Her hair was thinning and had gone a dirty yellow colour. Altogether, in that long moment of waiting, it seemed almost impossible that the creature in front of him could ever have been a woman for whom a man would ruin his life. The only scrap of comfort he could take was that a certain richness of red hair might, as its possessor aged, take on that particular shade of soiled yellow.

With a glance at her son, the old woman said at last, "My name is Bridget Crowe."

At that, McGuigan grunted and took the seat he had just vacated. With an easing of the shoulders that might have been the sketch of a shrug, Antony Crowe sat down opposite his mother.

"Was that your first marriage?"

"I was never married to Crowe," she said. "I've only been married once in my life."

Meldrum took a breath and put his intuition to the test. "Was that to Michael Thorne?" he asked.

"Is this about Michael?" she said in a kind of fright. "He's all right, isn't he?"

It was a shocking moment. Many times in his career, Meldrum had taken on the task of breaking a death to someone and not rarely it had been to the wife of a man who had died by violence, in a street fight or a pub brawl or something stranger. The task, though, had always been anticipated and, given the opportunity, he had known how to prepare himself for it. This time, sprung upon him, the need left him momentarily at a loss.

In any case, the hesitation had told her some part of the truth.

"He's not all right, is he?"

"I'm afraid he's dead," Meldrum said.

"We should have died together."

"Ah, come on now, mother," Crowe said, "that's no way to talk."

There was no reason to assume he wasn't sincere, but that didn't stop something in the cadence of the words falling unpleasantly on Meldrum's ear as if they were being offered from a stage.

"There was a time we thought we wouldn't be able to live if we were parted. And now he's dead?" She sounded puzzled by the awkward fact of it. "How did he die?"

Crowe spoke first. "He was murdered."

"And you knew it?" she asked her son.

220

"Why would I distress you by telling you? What good would that have done?"

"How could you think I wouldn't find out?"

He held up his hands, the forefingers pointed up as if to make a point with an opponent in an argument. Not heatedly, but mildly, he remonstrated, "When did you last speak of him? I'm not saying you didn't think about him. But isn't it true his name doesn't come up between us?"

"Not telling me wasn't right!"

"It would be different if he hadn't left you." In the same mild tone, he explained to the detectives, "He left her when I was born. It's true they got together again years later. He'd got married by then, and left his wife for her. She claims he married her then, but you might want to check and see if he ever got a divorce."

"You should be ashamed talking to me like that."

"If you knew anything about the police, you'd know they wouldn't need to be told. It's what they do. They're very keen on checking things."

"We were married in God's sight."

"Does that mean I wasn't a bastard any more?" He smiled at Meldrum. "Better late than never. Must have been about the time I was such a loser I joined the army. I wish I'd known."

The old woman's lips pressed together into a single bloodless line.

"I'll tell you why Michael Thorne left me. Not once but twice and the same reason both times." Her whole attention concentrated on him, it was as if she was alone with her son. "I'll tell you why he abandoned us and you only a baby. He left because God wanted him. He left God for me and in the end God called him back. He told me when he left he would never sleep with another woman but belong to God only until the day he died."

CHAPTER
FORTY-NINE

Sitting at the table in his flat, picking the last of the chips and white flakes of haddock in their clinging slither of batter from the greasy paper, Meldrum remembered McGuigan's question, "Why didn't you tell *us* who you were?" He would have been hard put to say why, but the memory of Crowe's answer made him smile: "You already had a son of Michael Thorne's to think about." And that was true. Colin Halliday had given them plenty to think about. Now with two sons things seemed likely to complicate even further. Never mind, the same unamused smile pulled at the corners of Meldrum's mouth, it had been satisfying to sense how thrown McGuigan had been by — what? intuition was altogether too fancy a term and anyway not accurate — by his *hunch* linking the cottage on the outskirts of Edinburgh in which Michael Thorne had told Mrs Halliday his lover Bridget lived with the cottage in which they'd interviewed Crowe and his mother. He hadn't even tried to explain to McGuigan how he'd made the connection, one which didn't seem to him abstruse since he had an old habit of holding everything around a crime in a kind of flux in his mind. The detective sergeant would have been even more upset if he had been tempted to explain all that to him, since the process would have made no sense to his own tidy linear habits of thought. For some time, Meldrum had been aware that McGuigan was well on the way to writing him off as a man past his peak. Upsetting for him to discover that the old man could still at moments recover a flair that the bright ambitious up-and-comer lacked. Call it a triumph then.

Not a big one, but call it a triumph.

As he was thinking that, his heart gave a leap as the knocker beat against the door that led out on to the common landing.

He was astonished to find the late night caller was his ex-wife Carole.

As he stood back, she came in and turned right into the sitting room. He was foolishly pleased that she remembered the way. There had been a time when she visited him in this flat. When they sold the bungalow, he had given most of the money to her and she had bought another place. With what was left, he'd put a deposit on a flat. He'd missed the garden of their bungalow at first, and when he first came to this flat in Leith Walk the ambulance and police sirens howling in the street below had disturbed him. Now he never heard them.

"I hate that close," Carole said. "Someone has spilled something disgusting on the landing and the stairs."

"Is something wrong with Betty or the baby?"

"Don't panic. Nobody's sick."

She picked the fish supper wrapping from where it lay on the cushion and put it on top of a pile of

224

outdated evening papers on the side table. Cautiously, she settled down as far from where the wrapping had been as she could manage.

"Could I have a cup of tea?" she asked. "Before we talk. I thought you'd be home earlier. Stupid of me. I should have known better."

On his way out into the lobby, he gathered up the greasy remnants of the fish supper and pushed them into the overflowing bin in the kitchen. It seemed strange to be making tea for her. They had married young and been very much in love. Even when the marriage broke up, some bond of affection had held them so that he would visit her in her new flat and they would talk about her profession as a head teacher in a primary school and, astonishingly, even about his own work, the endless hours of total commitment that had sucked the content out of their life together. He had never for a moment thought of marrying again, and it had come as a shock when Don Corrigan appeared on the scene. Since then, naturally, things could only be different between them.

When he came back with the tray, he realised that all the surfaces were covered and there was nowhere to put it. He set it down on the carpet and crouched beside it to pour the two cups. No need to ask if she wanted milk or sugar. He gave her the cup, and added milk and three sugars to his own before sitting on the chair opposite her.

"You're looking tired," he said, and was sorry at once.

She didn't seem upset, however, nodding as if it was too obviously the case to be worth a reaction. She was a woman who had kept her girlish good looks well into middle age, and it saddened him that time should be beginning to deal badly with her.

"Don doesn't know I'm here."

No surprise there. Corrigan disliked him as much as he despised Corrigan.

"Why should he?"

After all we're not going to jump into bed together, he thought, and was surprised by the thought and the stirring in his groin that came with it. She sat in silence then long enough for him to understand how lonely in fact he was.

At last, with a shake of the head, she said, "I came because I want you to stop Betty from going to America."

"Going where?" He stared at her in astonishment.

"She hasn't told you?" She sounded dismayed. "I thought — you two have always been so close — she hasn't discussed it? I even thought you might have encouraged her."

"She's got a job in America?"

"So she says."

"Tommy's too wee to go to America. Who'd look after him?"

"She's going without him."

"How can she do that?"

Suddenly she was angry with him. "By leaving him with me. How do you think? For God's sake, I'm her mother. Have you forgotten that?"

226

Fatally, then, he blurted out, "Leave wee Tommy with Don Corrigan? That's not right!"

"What kind of thing is that to say? What's it got to with Don? That's not why she shouldn't leave. It's for her own sake. She's not well enough to be on her own. Out there in a strange country. Anything could happen to her. *Don?*" The name came out as a kind of groan. "Is that all you can think of? I came here for help. What's happened to you?"

He had a long habit of self control. He drew on it to keep quiet. As a result the silence between them lengthened until, as with two strangers thrown together, it took on a quality not unlike embarrassment. Self control wasn't always the best solution.

At last he said, "I'll speak to her."

"Try to make her understand it's for her own good. I couldn't bear the thought of her being ill out there. It's not like this country. Unless you've money, they'd let you die in the street."

"I don't understand how she could leave the wee fellow." But he'd blundered already with that.

She said, "Don's fond of him. If you could see them together, you'd understand that."

Again he controlled himself. "That's not what I was thinking of," he said. "Doesn't a mother want to be with her child?"

"It's more complicated than that."

"It wasn't complicated for you. You wouldn't have left her when she was a toddler."

"That was different."

"How was it?"

"Oh, for God's sake!" She chopped at the air with her hand. It was a gesture of irritation barely suppressed that she had used a lot in the last days of their marriage. "I was married. She isn't, not any more. The baby was ours. She won't tell us who Tommy's father is. I'd never lost a child, I'd never had a dead child. I'd never been in a mental ward. Do you need any more?"

He felt as if he had been physically battered. All he could find to say was, "I don't understand her any more."

"No."

Though she didn't want him to, he insisted on seeing her downstairs and safely to her car. They went down in silence. As she skirted the stain splashed on the steps under the first landing, he saw the close through her eyes. He had left his flat door unlocked and hadn't brought keys, so he put the snib over on the close door to make sure it didn't lock behind him.

Out in the street, they walked slowly past the line of parked cars until she stopped beside hers. As she opened the door, he said, "I'll speak to her."

If he had hoped for a response, he would have been disappointed. Perhaps she felt there was nothing else to say. Perhaps from what he'd already said, she could foresee nothing but failure. Perhaps she wondered why she had come.

After she drove away, he stood for minutes on end looking after the car even when it had vanished from sight at the end of the street. When he understood what he was doing, it took a physical effort, as if shouldering

228

a weight, before he could bring himself to turn and make his way back.

As he climbed the stairs, he became conscious of the echo of feet on the flights below. A neighbour, someone with a key; but with the thought he wondered if he had taken off the snib to relock the street door. He couldn't remember. In fact, he had no memory of the time between watching the car leave and stepping on to his own landing. Tired to the bone, all he wanted to do was go in and sit down. In time, he would go to bed. For the moment, he was too tired for sleep.

He pushed open his door and had begun to go in when an instinct made him glance round.

Antony Crowe was hard on his heels.

CHAPTER
FIFTY

Meldrum was a man of some physical hardihood. Even in the moment of surprise, he didn't feel threatened. If he had, it would have been easy to react, slam the door or begin to shout. As it was, he simply rested in the surprise, trying to make sense of the man's unexpected appearance; even having time, in the way of the mind's untidy working, to put some of the blame on his omitting to lock the street door behind him.

As for Crowe, he succeeded in conveying passivity, hands dangling by his sides, a mild placatory smile fixed in place.

When he spoke, his voice was soft, almost wheedling.

"I've been struggling with my conscience," he said. "Would it be all right if we talked?"

Every reason in the world why not.

Why not? he decided.

Meldrum went back into the sitting room he'd left ten minutes earlier. He sat down in the chair he'd vacated. He heard the door being closed and then Crowe came in and without waiting to be asked sat on the couch. Meldrum noted that, not having the advantage Carole had possessed, Crowe settled himself on the spot where the fish supper had rested. It was a clue to his state of mind that he didn't find this amusing.

"I've come empty handed," Crowe said. "I'd a friend who was a picture dealer. He always took a bottle of whisky when he went visiting, especially if he was going to the monastery."

"I don't keep it in the house."

"That makes sense. Self discipline."

"If I kept it in the house," Meldrum said, "I'd drink it."

"That's something a lot of people wouldn't admit. I admire that. You're an unusually honest man."

Meldrum studied him. Unemotionally, he said, "I'm still trying to decide what kind of man you are."

"A man who'd like to help the police with the murder of his father."

"You took your time about coming forward."

Crowe shrugged. "My mother. I explained that."

"But you *are* Michael Thorne's son?"

"Unacknowledged." He made a meal of the word. "He took fright, you know. Went to his bishop and threw himself on the ample mercy of the Church. I was ripped, if not untimely from my mother's womb, from her arms." He paused, like a witness being scrupulous in correcting his evidence. "I don't know, in fact, if she ever held me. My earliest memory is of being in a Home run by nuns. Unfortunate women demented by celibacy. Not having that insight as a child, I saw them simply as monsters. Does this interest you?"

Did it? Of course, it should. In a long career, Meldrum had never sat in his own home with someone involved, in some way, surely in some way, however innocently, in a murder he was investigating. He was held, however, in the grip of a lethargy of the spirit more disabling than physical exhaustion.

Gathering his thoughts, he said, "By your own account, you were taken away at birth more or less. When did you make contact again with your mother?"

"I've led a strange life," Crowe said. "The third foster parents I had, when they emigrated to New Zealand took me along with them. No right to, but it's amazing what people can get away with when they don't care. I was there for four years before I ran away. I arrived back on my fifteenth birthday and it was snowing. Welcome home. They don't have snow in New Zealand. Not even in the North Island, except for Mount Ruapehu and Mount Ngauruhoe and on the desert roads. Did you know that?"

Apart from holidays, which he had never enjoyed taking, and the occasional police business, Meldrum had hardly been out of Scotland in his life.

"That's when you went looking for your mother?"

"No. I didn't give her a thought for years." He paused and then corrected himself, the meticulous witness again. "That's not true. I thought about her." From the look on his face, not necessarily pleasantly. "But I was on my own. The first order of business was living. After a bit, I joined the army. I was in the Falklands. Later on, in the first Gulf War."

Looking at the hard reckless face, Meldrum asked, "Were you ever in trouble with the police?"

"Before I went into the army. Nothing serious. If you've no money and no home, the police take an interest."

"Policemen aren't social workers. They take an interest when you break the law."

(The following day, Meldrum instigated a records search. There was no trace of an Antony Crowe being convicted of any offence in the Seventies or during the time he claimed to have been in the army.)

"I came out of the army in '94. Went in a boy and came out a man, isn't that what they say? I was at a bit of a loss, though. They'd taught me to kill people, but that isn't a trade. Would it be cheeky if I asked for a cup of tea?"

They both looked at the tray still sitting on the carpet. Later, Meldrum decided this was a turning point. Instead of throwing Crowe out, he made tea.

Seated again, he looked at Crowe over his cup and asked as he drank, "About your mother?"

"If you want to find out about your biological parent, it isn't hard now. There's a law says you have to be told. I traced her to that cottage. She was living with this man Crowe. He died not long afterwards and I moved in to keep her company."

"Why change your name?"

"To Crowe? I liked the sound of it."

"Was there a reason why you didn't call yourself Thorne? Once you knew he was your father. Assuming that is you felt you had to change your name at all."

"The police weren't looking for me, if that's what you mean." He laughed. "Or men with baseball bats, either!"

"I was thinking more about meeting your father. You did meet Michael Thorne?"

Crowe tipped up the cup and drank. "Do you mind?" He nodded at the pot on the tray. Getting down as Meldrum had done earlier, he poured himself another cup. Meldrum, who had no desire for more, was struck all the same by the fact that it didn't seem even to occur to Crowe to offer to pour for him as well.

Crowe sat down again and sipped at the tea before nodding as if to himself. "You're very good," he said, as if confirming a verdict. "After my mother told me about how they had met; how I had been conceived — I don't mean the details, for a woman with a great love affair, she's quite prudish. The priest and the temptress, eh? I'd have been made of stone not to go and see him for myself. Having met him, I didn't feel like calling myself Thorne. It gave me pleasure to tell him I'd decided on Crowe."

"Did you hate him?"

"For walking out on my mother? Bit late for that. Put it this way, he was a disappointment. When you don't know who your father is, you imagine someone very special. A good man or a bad one matters less than that he should be a *big* man. Not an old smelly left over." He shuddered with what looked like real fastidiousness. "Did you hear my mother talking about how he left her because God was calling him? She refused to listen to me when I told her he slept with women. He didn't have any inhibitions about talking freely to me. Why should he? He was lonely. And still my mother comes away with that garbage about him vowing never to sleep with another woman. She does it to annoy me."

"My impression," Meldrum said, "was that she believed what she was saying."

"Or maybe she thinks prostitutes don't count! Could that be it?" He laughed. "From what they tell me, not many women believe that. On the other hand, plenty of men do, wouldn't you say?"

"I suppose, it's a matter of conscience."

"What I told you I was wrestling with?"

"You're quick," Meldrum said. And he, according to Crowe, was honest. A mutual admiration society.

"I didn't come to see you in your office deliberately. I didn't want to meet you as a policeman. I saw something in you. I wanted to talk to you as a man." Crowe leaned forward. "I'm putting myself in your hands."

"I'm always a policeman," Meldrum said.

"Maybe I should just get up and go away."

Meldrum gave a humourless smile. "If you think you can leave it at that, you don't know much about policemen."

"How persuasive you are. In your hands then," he repeated. "I believe my father was killed because of something he knew. You talk about me being slow to come forward. I have to tell you it isn't easy for me to be here. If you ask me why I am, all I can say to you is conscience."

"How much of that does it take? Most men would want to catch their father's killer."

Crowe frowned. "Have you been listening? Most men? You think Thorne treated me like a son? That he's what most men think of as *Daddy*?" He drew out the last word as a sneer.

"The idea of him mattered enough for you to go looking for him."

"If I'm right, it would be safer for me not to be involved."

"Safer?"

"Involved at all in the matter of his death. It may be that I've already put myself in danger. They must be aware that I got to know my father before his death. As far as they were concerned, I must have appeared from nowhere. It's just possible they might not know I was his son, though it seems a long shot. If they do know, they're bound to assume he confided in me. From their point of view, talking to the police would confirm that." He smiled. "Another reason for coming here to talk to you."

"They? Did I miss something?"

"If you expect me to give names and addresses, I'll disappoint you. All I can tell you is that my father had got himself mixed up in something dangerous. He had obtained knowledge of a conspiracy. That's how he described it to me, 'a conspiracy'. Even speaking of it frightened him. Of course, I tried to get him to say more. A massive conspiracy was all he would add. Something, he claimed, that could alter the history of the world."

"In Edinburgh?" Meldrum wondered. His tone was dry. He had the typical reaction of his countrymen, one of the debilitating results of three hundred years of lost independence, that nothing important could happen in Scotland.

"Wider than that," Crowe said seriously. "Wider than these islands. Wider, he hinted, than Europe."

Meldrum's first thought was that this was an attempt by the man to divert attention from himself, the paradoxical effect of which, of course, was to make him a prime object of suspicion.

"No harm to your father," he said, "but from what I saw of his flat, the way he lived, an old man on his own, it's hard to believe he'd know about anything as big as that."

"My reaction wasn't different. I said as much. That made him angry. It goaded him into telling me that as a young priest he'd been in a group of the faithful, priests and laymen, with members all over the world. 'I was regarded as brilliant then,' he told me."

"That doesn't sound ordinary to me. You talked about being disappointed in your father because he was an ordinary man."

Crowe's expression didn't change, but he sat unmoving and silent long enough for Meldrum to feel that he had scored a hit. At last he said, "Vanity is ordinary enough. It was that vanity, though, that made me take him seriously. He told me there were two sides. The members of the conspiracy and this brotherhood of his. The sacred task of the brotherhood was to thwart the conspirators. Two groups spread across the world.

At that point, he broke off as if he'd gone too far, and I couldn't get him to tell me any more."

"What a pity," Meldrum said, in the tone of careful neutrality he so often adopted. "In that case, there wouldn't be any point in trying to pursue it. He left it too vague."

"You're forgetting something," Crowe said. "He didn't just have one son, he had *two*. He'd known the other one as many years as he knew me months. If he told me as much as he did, I'm sure he told Colin Halliday more."

"You want me to try out this story on Colin Halliday?"

"And I can tell you where to start. Ask him about the Fatima Project."

"Fatima?"

"The name means something to you?"

Meldrum shook his head. "I've read it somewhere."

"Ask Colin Halliday."

When Crowe took himself off, he left abruptly. Getting up in the middle of a sentence as if summoned, he was gone with hardly a word. Meldrum didn't see him out, but sat on after he'd heard the door close out in the lobby. He thought about getting a beer, then sipped instead at the tea left in his cup. It had gone cold but, a slow drinker, more than half the tea he'd drunk in his life had been cold.

In the night, he woke and lay thinking how grey his existence was and how much more interesting life would be if a story like Crowe's of a conspiracy that might reshape the world could possibly be true.

CHAPTER
FIFTY-ONE

"You can afford it," Detective Sergeant Terry Porter suggested. He was talking of the restaurant to which Meldrum had taken him for lunch. "What are you on — top of the scale — 43 K?"

Porter was a round-faced, balding fifty-year-old with a strong Manchester accent and a private life that included a regular commitment as a Baptist lay preacher. Meldrum had made his acquaintance six years earlier when he'd had to spend time in the English city in pursuit of an inquiry. The Mancunian had impressed him professionally by his shrewdness and that, together with an unusual impression of quiet balance, had led to the two men getting on exceptionally well, not a common experience for Meldrum. That morning they had renewed their friendship, this time because Porter had arrived to take a suspect back south with him. In defiance of the files on his desk, the hovering McGuigan and all he had to do urgently, Meldrum had taken him off to lunch.

If Porter was flattered, he was also puzzled. The restaurant was just too good. They were on to the main course before Meldrum brought himself to the point.

"Can I ask you something?"

Porter chewed contentedly on a mouthful of steak and nodded. "You want to join the big time? I'll put in a word for you in Manchester if you want."

"Aye, and pigs'll fly. It's kind of private. I need somebody to talk to that . . ." He trailed off, trying to work it out.

"Somebody that's going to be off south and out of your life this afternoon."

Relieved at this further proof of his companion's shrewdness, Meldrum said, "That's it actually."

"Fine," Porter said. "I've no problem with that. There are only two kinds of people you can talk to about something private. Friends you'd trust with your life and guys that you meet on the train. Somebody that'll be on a plane this afternoon is nearly as good." Fishing with his tongue, he drew down a string of fibre from between his front teeth. "Fire away."

"This friend of mine," Meldrum began and paused at the sharp-eyed glance of amused scepticism that opening brought. Paused, but repeated himself; if it was a fiction acknowledged by them both it was one he wanted to maintain. "This friend of mine." Point made, he ploughed on. "He was married. Got divorced. Nobody's fault. Not hers anyway. Call it the job."

"This bloody job."

"The two of them stayed friends. He'd drop in to see her sometimes. He still found it easier to talk to her than anyone else. Did I say they'd a daughter? She wasn't a kid, she was grown up, got married herself and had a baby. She was the one that told him he wasn't being fair. Going to see her mother all the time, she meant. You're not being fair to her, she said. That took him aback. Next thing, his wife —"

"Ex-wife?"

"Ex-wife announced she was getting married again."

"It happens."

"Thing is, just about then this friend of mine had a case, a pro who was killed. And she kept a book with her clients and their tastes. And he was in it, the new husband. Maybe he should have gone to the wife and told her. Just gone, not thought about it, just gone and told her. But he didn't."

"Just as well," Porter said seriously. "He'd have been crossing the line."

"Don't worry, he didn't. But he did tell the husband."

"Bloody fool! Worst of both worlds."

Meldrum grunted agreement. "He wasn't thinking straight."

"When did all this happen?"

"A while ago."

Finished, Porter laid his knife and fork side by side and pushed the plate away. "There you go then. Time to forget about it."

"It isn't that easy."

"If you're asking for my advice, make it easy. Doesn't matter how much you love a woman. When it's over, you have to know it's over."

Meldrum made a movement of impatience. Who was talking about love? Did this stupid bastard think he would come whining to him about love?

"I told you there was a married daughter. She'd a baby that died. They had another one and then the husband left her. The baby wasn't his. Since then the baby and her have been living with her mother and the father-in-law. As for my friend, the father-in-law doesn't even want him in the house. He can't even see his grandson!"

"Tough," Porter said. "Just one of those things you have to live with."

"Aye, but now the daughter wants to go to the States. She's got a job out there." Ambushed by his bitterness, he burst out, "How could a mother go and leave her baby? I don't understand that."

"Grannies looking after kids. It's not the end of the world. I wouldn't blame her too much."

"But she's not just leaving the wee fellow with her mother, she's leaving him with that bloody pervert as well. That's not right. That can't be right. I should do something about it. My friend should do something about it."

"What? Like tell his ex-wife? If he was going to do that, he should have done it at the time. Too late now."

Perhaps because it wasn't what he'd wanted to hear, Meldrum sensed something complacent, even patronising, in this advice.

"Anyway," Porter said, "because a guy is kinky with a pro doesn't mean he's a bad man, he might be great with the kid."

Since this drew no response, they sat with their own thoughts until the coffee arrived, after what seemed to Meldrum an unconscionably long wait.

242

"This bloody job," Porter broke his silence. "It's a young man's game. I'll be retired next year. I'm looking forward to doing the allotment. Having time in the morning to read the paper and do the Sudoku. What about you?"

If there was one thing Meldrum hated more than another, it was talk of retirement. He stirred the sugar in his coffee, watched the whirlpool while he thought about it.

Finally he asked, "What the hell's Sudoku?"

CHAPTER
FIFTY-TWO

Meldrum wasn't a great dreamer. Once, after a bone graft for a nasty shoulder break, he'd been attached for a night to a morphine pump. Next morning the man in the opposite bed, who'd also been self administering morphine all night, had asked if he'd had his blood replaced yet. On being told he didn't think so, the man had explained that he'd have been in no doubt, since when the blood lost during an operation was pumped back in later: "you can hear the whirring at the end of the bed where they attach the machine for sterilising it." In place of such lively fantasies, Meldrum had enjoyed during the hours of darkness only an impression of his thoughts moving very easily, as if the parts of a machine had been greased.

Three nights after the unexpected visit to his flat, however, just before dawn, Meldrum vividly saw Crowe's face leaning over him as he said, "Harmless theft. I was a boy alone in the world. Who would blame me?" And woke to realise it was a dream.

He'd already had the records searched for the Seventies through the early Eighties without finding any convictions against Antony Crowe. After his dream, however, as though it had been sent to him as a

244

reminder of the obvious, he realised that the man wouldn't have been calling himself Crowe then, since it would be before he'd even heard of his mother's latest partner. Assuming that some time after he'd come back from New Zealand, the boy had found the name of his real mother, Meldrum ran a second check on the records, this time for an Antony O'Neill; and there he was — convicted of assault in '75, theft in '78, attempted rape in 1980. Not a past that would have made him a welcome recruit into the army, and so presumably he'd faked his record. After finding an army discharge, an honourable one, in '94, on impulse he ran a second check and found Antony O'Neill had been convicted of armed robbery in September '95, a year after leaving the army. He had been sentenced to eight years, but had been at liberty again by the end of '98.

With the material in front of him on the desk, Meldrum wondered what had made him so slow about getting on the trail. Untypically, the notion occurred to him that perhaps unconsciously he hadn't wanted to find out the truth about the charismatic Crowe: that he was the youthful thug O'Neill made over by a spell in the army into an armed robber. What was the slogan? Join the army and learn a trade. Apart from killing people, of course.

Nothing else on his record, though, after that robbery conviction. Presumably it had been shortly after getting out of prison in '98 that he'd sought out his mother. Had her influence kept him on the straight and narrow ever since? *Had* he been on the straight and

245

narrow ever since? And what about the mother's partner, the man called Crowe? Hadn't he died not long after her son had traced her to the cottage outside Edinburgh?

Hurrying since, immersed in the records, he'd kept the team waiting, he was brought to a halt at the door of the incident room by the unexpected sound of laughter. No surprise that it was Sharkey who was in full flow. "I blame all these TV shows. Calls himself a policeman. A grown bloody man and he's nearly greeting, telling us his wife is going with a younger man. Too much bloody information. I couldn't believe my ears. 'What am I going to do?' he's asking the three of us. And the wife's a lot younger than him, which doesn't help matters. Young lovers! But I know him. You're so bloody competitive, I say to him, just tell her, Right, bitch! That's us up to *twice* a year!"

Even the dour McGuigan was managing a thin reluctant smile until he caught sight of him listening in the doorway. As he made his way to the front of the room, the laughter trailed into silence.

"Three bodies," he said. "Michael Thorne. Shona Flett. Nicholas Aaron. Forensics connects them. Nothing in Aaron's life connects him to the other two. We've got a serial killer on our hands." He looked round slowly. Sandy MacIntosh, rubbing his long nose, Fred Houston running a finger under his collar, Eddie Sharkey, not smiling now, Melrose, Petrie, Lang. None of them, not even McGuigan, meeting his eye. "Let me put it this way," he said, "the joke's fucking over." He held up the photograph of the missing student. "Keeley Robertson. We've a witness who identifies her as the woman Aaron left the hotel with. We need to find her."

CHAPTER
FIFTY-THREE

Although Meldrum had a strong desire to see Colin Halliday, there was only one destination that made sense that morning after a final check through the records.

The sky over the Forth was making a decision for blue, the last of the early grey clouds thinning and blowing away to the northeast as they ran along the A1. To their left they could see the floodlights for the extension of the racecourse at Musselburgh. Just beyond it, the skeleton of the stand for the new greyhound track was taking shape.

"Are we going to arrest him?" McGuigan asked, breaking the silence that had held since they got into the car.

"Shouldn't think so. Depends on how he reacts."

"I could crack him. I'd bet he's not as tough as he looks."

"You a betting man?"

"What do you mean?"

"If you were, I'd stick to the horses."

McGuigan pressed the button and the window slid down. When it was low enough, he hawked and spat out into the slipstream. It was one way of conveying the sentiment *fuck-you-too*.

Ten minutes later, they were parking outside the cottage beside the little factory. Sunlight sparkled through raindrops on the barbed wire of the factory fence.

As they turned into the path, they saw Antony Crowe with his back to them locking the door. Whatever small noise they made, he turned fast as a cat. If he was startled at seeing them, his face gave nothing away.

"You're lucky," he said. "Five minutes later and I'd have been away." He gestured and they saw he was holding two bottles of wine in the fingers of his free hand. "I was taking some people a treat. Going to stop on the way for a big box of chocolates. Put a towel on my head and I'd be the Good Samaritan."

"Would you mind going back inside with us, sir?" McGuigan asked.

Watching Crowe's eyes narrow, Meldrum wondered if he too had caught the undercurrent of triumph in the sergeant's voice.

In the shadowy front room, Meldrum took a seat without being asked. Though it might once have been comfortable, the cloth on the arms was worn, and the cushion had sunk leaving a ridge of wood that gouged into the backs of his thighs. Not wanting to admit his mistake by getting up, or too weary to care, he lounged back like a spectator at a wrestling match looking up as the other two confronted one another.

"Is your mother home, Mr O'Neill?" McGuigan asked.

"If you want to talk to me, use my name."

Was that edge in his voice anger? Faint, if so, but enough from so self-controlled a man to make the spectator's muscles tighten involuntarily.

"Would you ask your mother to join us, Mr Crowe?"

"Why?"

"It would save time if she had to confirm anything for you."

"Is this about Shona Flett? Because she put me in her will?"

"It could be," McGuigan said. "We're still wondering why she did that. Or maybe about something else."

"If you've anything to ask me, get on with it."

"And your mother?"

"Sleeping."

"If you say so." McGuigan let a minute of silence pass before he went on, "Let me run some dates past you. Stop me, if you recognise any of them. January 24, 1975. July 10, 1978. November 11, 1980."

In his turn, Crowe was silent for a moment. When he laughed, the effect was shocking, not least because the laughter seemed spontaneous. "Let me run some names past you," he said, parodying the sergeant's tone. "Edward Fisher. Willie Aitken. Nettie Faulds. You recognise them? You should, you look like a man who does his homework." He looked down at Meldrum. "What about you? Or is the organ grinder going to leave it to the monkey?"

Meldrum got to his feet. As he did, the other two visibly braced themselves.

"Now you've inherited money," he said, "you should get yourself some comfortable chairs." In the same mild, almost indifferent tone, he went on, "Edward Fisher was the man you assaulted in '75."

"I was seventeen," Crowe said. "No one in the world to look after me except myself."

"Fisher was a man in his sixties."

"He should have had more sense then, but he'd drunk enough to think he was a hero. I punched him once in the face and ran off without his wallet, which was all I'd wanted in the first place. As I say, just a kid."

"You broke his nose and his cheekbone."

"My fist must have bounced. Anyway two policemen were waiting round the corner."

Because you'd done it before, Meldrum thought; rolled drunks outside a pub. He decided against pursuing that, asking instead, "And Willie Aitken?"

"It wasn't Fort Knox. A wee shop that sold papers and cigarettes. Capstan, Pall Mall, Woodbine. I reached over the counter when he rang up the till. Got a handful of notes. Not exactly a master criminal."

"You were twenty-two when you were up for rape," McGuigan said. "I don't call that being a kid."

"You're embarrassing me," Crowe said easily. "The old bitch was twice twenty-two and then probably another few on top. She was on the game. The thought of her turns my stomach now. As a matter of fact, it did then too. I told her I'd changed my mind, but she still wanted her money."

"The records must have got it wrong then," Meldrum said. "They have Nettie Faulds down as sixteen. And they don't say anything about being on the game."

He felt oddly disappointed with this resort to barefaced, easily disproved lying. He'd thought there was more to Crowe than that.

As if reading his thoughts, Crowe said, "I've always had a good imagination. Does it matter? That stuff was a long time ago. I'm not the person I was then."

"You want it more up to date?" McGuigan asked. "Try July 28, 1995."

"Try armed robbery at a bookies in Glasgow," Meldrum said.

"I wasn't the one with the gun."

"It's still a jump from robbing sweetie shops."

"Not sweeties; papers and cigarettes," Crowe said, the pleasure of contradiction seeming to relax him for he smiled as he continued, "I fell into bad company. Two old comrades from my time in the Army. We were in Desert Storm together."

"That's an excuse?" McGuigan asked with a sneer.

"I haven't been in trouble since. All the wild oats sown. My mother's been a good influence on me."

Behind him, the door swung wide and Bridget O'Neill gaped at the sight of the three men seeming to fill the room in front of her.

"What's wrong?" she asked, her voice thin with shock.

McGuigan reacted first. He stepped aside saying, "Have a seat."

She looked at Crowe, who shrugged. "Why not?" he said.

252

As she sat down, the men also seated themselves so that in a moment the group had taken on the appearance of taking part in an ordinary conversation.

"You were here before," she said, looking at the two detectives. "I told you that Antony was at home when that woman was killed."

"What about the night your partner Peter Crowe died?" McGuigan asked.

The question coming so soon and so baldly took Meldrum by surprise so that he missed the first instant of Crowe's reaction to it.

"Antony didn't live here then."

"We know he didn't come to stay with you until after your partner's death," Meldrum said. "But before that he'd already been to see you."

"After he came out of prison in August, 1998," McGuigan said.

"It was a wonderful surprise," the old woman said. As she went on, Crowe began a kind of tuneless humming. "I opened the door and there he was. There had never been a day that passed when I didn't think of the baby I'd lost. When I saw what a fine man he'd grown into, I thought, I don't have to feel guilty any more."

"Was your partner there when your son turned up?" McGuigan asked.

She put her hand over her mouth. "Oh, no," she said.

"Oh, yes," Crowe echoed her with an effect like mockery. "He was there all right. Sitting in that chair you're in, sergeant. From the beer gut, I'd guess he spent a lot of time on his arse."

253

"Did you quarrel with him?"

"It wasn't him I was here to see."

"But you didn't like him?"

"How can I put it?" Crowe asked. "He made me wonder about my mother's taste in men."

"You weren't sorry then to hear he'd died." McGuigan made it more of a statement than a question.

"My mother was upset. That's why I came to stay with her." He smiled. "Isn't that what sons do?"

"The thing is," Meldrum said, "when you told us about his death before, we took it for granted that he'd died of natural causes."

"He was found beaten to death," Crowe said.

McGuigan leaned forward. "That would be about a week after you made contact with your mother."

"Life's full of coincidences."

"I don't know what I'd have done on my own," the mother said. "I'd have had no one to turn to. Thank God you were here."

"Do you remember where you were the night he died?" McGuigan asked.

"Normally I'd say no. It was a long time ago. But it so happens I was spending that night with a friend. During the evening, I phoned to see how my mother was getting on and she told me what had happened. I was shocked, of course."

"Could you give us the name of this friend?"

"Shona Flett."

"Shona Flett?" McGuigan drawled disbelievingly.

"Hmm. As a witness, she has the disadvantage of being dead. But I can only tell you what happened," Crowe said. "She was with me when I heard Peter Crowe had been beaten to death outside his favourite pub."

"And after that, you started to call yourself Antony Crowe," Meldrum said.

Crowe nodded and, reaching over, patted his mother's hand.

Discomfited, Meldrum saw the old woman clasp his hand in both of hers and that as she smiled at him she had tears in her eyes.

Later, as he saw them out, Crowe laid his hand on Meldrum's arm.

"Coming here to rake up the past. I'm not surprised at your sergeant, but I'd thought better of you."

With a jerk, Meldrum pulled his arm free. "Go to hell," he said, the strength of his reaction taking him by surprise before he could monitor his response.

McGuigan, who was already half way down the path, looked back at the sound of the raised voice.

"I don't blame you for being in a hurry to get away." Crowe spoke loudly enough to be heard by both men. "The stink of an old woman. It's not pleasant, is it? And yet, I have it in my nostrils all day."

With that, he stepped back inside and closed the door.

CHAPTER
FIFTY-FOUR

"Project?" Colin Halliday said. "Legend. Miracle. Revelation. Call it any of those. The Legend of Fatima. Or the Miracle. But I don't understand why anyone would talk about a *Project*."

Meldrum didn't answer at once, intrigued by the sweat that had suddenly appeared on Halliday's forehead. Just under the hairline, a coating of fine drops were caught in the sunlight from the window of the seminar room.

"That was the term he used."

"Antony Crowe?"

"Your landlord."

"But I hardly know him. He came here after Shona's death, but just to talk about the flat. He wants to sell it at some point."

"And you can't think of any reason why he would suggest that I ask you about this Fatima thing, whatever it is?"

"If you'd raised the topic for some reason, he might have thought of me. After all, he knows that I lecture on religion."

"It has to do with religion?"

"But of course." He seemed to relax. "Is this just to satisfy your own curiosity? Is that why you came on your own?"

"Why don't we sit down and you can tell me about it?"

"I really don't have much time. I'm going out this evening to visit friends."

"Is that what the wine is for?" Two bottles of wine stood beside the coat Halliday had thrown across his desk. When a nod confirmed this guess, he went on, "There's a coincidence. When I saw Crowe this morning, he was on his way to visit friends. He had bottles of wine — oh, and he was going to buy chocolates. So that would be women friends, eh?"

"I told you I hardly know the man!" Halliday said, and seated himself at once as if as a kind of distraction from having made the point too emphatically.

"Fatima?" Meldrum said, following suit.

"It's a small town in Portugal. The year before the First World War ended, the Virgin Mary appeared as an apparition to three peasant children, two little girls and a boy. They had taken their flock of sheep to graze on pasture in a natural hollow just outside the town. The older girl was called Jacinta. Can't remember the other two children." He got up and fetched a book from the reference shelf in the corner. Thumbing through it, he paused and said, "Here we are. I was wrong. Lucia was the oldest. She was ten. She was with her two cousins, Francisco, who was eight, and Jacinta, seven. They were herding their sheep when there was a flash of lightning and a — I quote — 'beautiful lady stood a few yards away. She gave off a dazzling light so that the children could hardly bear to keep their eyes on her. Lucia, the oldest child, got up the courage to ask, "Where are you from?" "I am from Heaven," came the answer. The children were told to return to the same place at the same time in the following months when she would appear to them again. In the meantime, they were to recite the rosary daily. She then rose in a cloud of light and glided away into the sky towards the east.' Had enough?" He went to lay the book aside.

Meldrum had been surprised by the nature of this Fatima story, but if he was no expert on the symbols of religion he had spent a long time learning to read those signs by which people gave away their unease or tension.

"Don't stop," he said.

Halliday shrugged. "Fine. Lucia had warned her cousins to say nothing about what had happened, but Jacinta, who was only seven, couldn't keep it to herself. Everyone thought the children were telling lies. Lucia's mother in particular punished her over and over again trying to get her to deny what she claimed to have seen. Other children spat on them and mocked them. But the Virgin kept her word, and scepticism gave way to belief," he smiled, "as it has a habit of doing among the peasantry. You're not a Catholic yourself?"

Meldrum shook his head.

"I wondered if that was why . . . Oh, well. By the time Our Lady appeared in October, there was a great crowd there to witness not only the Appearance but the miracle of the sun whirling from the heavens and

258

dancing down towards the children, changing colours as it came, all the colours of the rainbow, until it settled briefly among the trees. This was seen over an area of thirty-two miles by twenty — over six hundred square miles." He paused as if waiting for some kind of comment on that claim, but Meldrum kept silent. "From here on it is Lucia's story. The two younger children died in the influenza pandemic that swept across the world just after the war ended. Lucia found a vocation as a Carmelite nun and became the source for the secrets, which the Virgin had entrusted to the children. There were three of them. The first began with a vision of hell and contained the prophecy that the Great War would soon end — as, of course, it did in the following year, 1918. The second secret was less predictable for it foresaw that Russia would 'spread her errors' across the world. According to Lucia, the Virgin told them, 'I shall come to ask for the consecration of Russia to My Immaculate Heart' and 'If people attend to My requests, Russia will be converted and the world will have peace.' Some people interpret Pope John Paul II's 1984 consecration of Russia as an attempt to obey that request and, of course, see it as leading to the collapse of the Soviet Union and the return of Russia to the fold of Christianity." Halliday looked up and pulled a sour face. "Whether that has produced a world at peace is a different question."

Halliday closed the book and looked expectantly at his coat with the two wine bottles beside it.

Instead of taking the hint, Meldrum asked, "And the third secret?"

Halliday sighed. "She wrote that one down and gave it to the local Bishop with instructions it wasn't to be opened till 1960. The Bishop passed it on to the Vatican. But when Pope John XXIII opened it in 1960, he refused to reveal the secret, giving as his reason, 'This prophecy doesn't relate to my time.' That's when the speculation began. One favourite was that the third secret told how the world would end and gave the date when it would happen. Another was that it foretold a schism in the Church that would lead to rival papacies. With that kind of expectation, there was a feeling of being let down when, at the beatification of Jacinta and Francisco in 2000, the Vatican secretary of state announced that the third secret was a prophecy of the attempt on Pope John Paul II's life in 1982. By 2000, that wasn't a prophecy about the future but a gloss on a past event. People asked why had it been kept until then; why not reveal it after the assassination attempt? A few years later, Lucia died in her convent at the age of ninety-seven. And that really is the best I can do for you."

Meldrum stared at him thoughtfully. "You tell a good story," he said.

"It's my job, part of my job."

"You've never talked about any of this with Crowe?"

"Hardly."

"I wonder why he wanted me to ask you about it."

Halliday got up and replaced the book on the shelf. Without looking round, he said something, so softly that it took Meldrum a moment to work out that he had muttered, "God only knows."

CHAPTER
FIFTY-FIVE

When Cadoc got to the house, the women were already sparkling-eyed and flushed. He sat the two bottles of wine on the sideboard and noted that the bottles already there were empty.

"At last," Grania said, laughing.

"You," the Convenor said, "would be late for your own funeral."

What, Cadoc wondered, was making the women so concentrated, so merry, so *alive*. More, surely, than three or four glasses of wine. His nostrils sipped at the air, warm since the Convenor had lit a huge fire in the open grate. (What had he used for fuel? Had he chopped up chairs or broken one of those ancient wardrobes in the upstairs bedrooms into walnut logs and bundles of firewood?) Was there a smell hanging in that warm air of musk, of damp crotches, of parted thighs? Had he taken them to bed? Which one first? Grania with her heavy breasts that seemed to move a beat more slowly as she turned? Emer, red hair loosened and flowing down over her shoulders? Grania with that air of middle-class assurance, whatever went wrong in her life it had begun in a house where bills were paid, cruises taken, careers spread out for the school leaver like a winning hand of cards. Emer, so young, so beautiful, but with that vulnerability as from a hidden wound which drew the predators to her. Which one first? Had the other waited, knowing she would be next? Had he taken them to bed *together*?

"I've never known what that meant. If it was my funeral, I would be the guest of honour. How could it start without me?"

"It wouldn't," Grania said; this time her laughter shriller, reminiscent to his raw nerves of the noise he sometimes made in the seminar room when the chalk rubbed the blackboard the wrong way. "It wouldn't start at all. They'd all have got bored and gone home."

"I was held up. I was going to put my coat on and leave, when someone turned up to ask me about what he called the Fatima Project."

"Oh God," Grania said. All the life drained from her face.

"Who was he?" Emer cried in fright.

"And what did you tell him?" the Convenor asked.

Cadoc looked at the three of them. The women each with her wide eyes and scarlet gash for a mouth, the Convenor lying back in the chair nearest the roaring fire, legs sprawled apart, a glass of wine balanced on his stomach. They were strangers to him. What was he doing here?

Cadoc, eyes on the younger woman, said cruelly, "He was a policeman." Turning to the Convenor, he said, "He asked about the Fatima Project. I told him, call it a miracle or a vision, project makes no sense. And then I went through it all, from the Virgin appearing to the children all the way through to Cardinal Sodano in 2000 when he claimed to reveal the third secret to the pilgrims at the beatification of Francisco and Jacinta."

"What did he say?"

"That I told a good story."

"I like that." The Convenor's tone was casual, almost amused. "He's an interesting man. Not your usual plod."

"Who?" Grania asked, her voice sharper still with a note of hysteria ready to surface. "Who are you talking about? What policeman?"

"I take it," the Convenor said, "it was Meldrum."

"Yes." *You know it was. You were the one who told him to ask me about the Project.* Cadoc wondered why that hadn't been his answer. It wasn't just that he was afraid of the Convenor, though he was mortally afraid of him. The truth was worse than that. He wanted them to be in collusion. He needed to feel that the two of them shared a secret that excluded the women. Needed to feel that, even if he himself had no real grasp of what the secret might be.

"The policeman who's investigating poor Bryd's death," the Convenor explained.

"For God's sake!" Grania cried. "Aren't we past that? I'm Sandra! She's Keeley! And it's Shona who's dead. Shona! not some stupid Celtic goddess."

At that, the room exploded. "Stupid cunt!" As the Convenor sat up, the glass of wine rolled from his chest smearing a blood-coloured trail across his shirt. He came up to his feet effortlessly, took two long strides and had slapped her across the face before the others knew what was happening. "You're whatever I fucking say you are."

In the appalled silence, Cadoc could hear the breath bubbling in the woman's nostrils and in his confusion thought for an instant that the threads running from her nose were nothing worse than spilled wine.

Keeley Robertson had slipped from her chair to the floor and with her hands over her face was crying a single word over and over again: "EmerEmerEmer."

And the Convenor began to laugh. "Keeley," he said. "Sit up and don't be silly." Tenderly he wiped the blood from the older woman's face. "No harm done, Sandra. Colin, open the wine you brought. This is supposed to be a party."

His control over them was such that in moments they were sitting again, each with a full glass in hand, as he set himself to making the tension leave their muscles and even succeeded in coaxing smiles from them, smiles to which he responded in turn so that each of them felt for that moment the sole focus of his attention.

When he had created the atmosphere he wanted, he said, "My coat's hanging in the hall, Colin. Fetch me the newspaper — it's in the left hand pocket."

Had there been some subtle change of tone? The two women sank into a silence, in which they were immersed until Halliday came back.

"I didn't want," Crowe said, "to show you this until we were all here."

264

The paper had been rolled into a tube and then cracked over to fit into his pocket. As he restored its original shape, they recognised it as the Edinburgh evening paper, presumably in an early or special edition.

To Sandra, late Grania, he said, "Discipline is going to be more important than ever now. If you didn't realise before how near we are to the brink — *I* didn't know, I thought I did but I didn't know the half of it — then this should convince you. We took out one of theirs, but see how they've taken out one of ours. We're fighting for our lives now."

He spread the paper out and rubbed his hand over it in an ironing motion. When he was satisfied, he held it up so that they could see the front page. The headline ran across the width of the sheet in black blocky lettering — **DEATH OF AN ASYLUM SEEKER**.

As Colin Halliday listened while it was explained how wrongly the paper read the event — did a newspaper ever give more than a misleading fraction of the truth? — how the dead man was a messenger who had been sent to warn them and been intercepted by the emissaries of the dark conspiracy against which they struggled, how much greater their danger had become, how much less their chances of success, how important it was that they did not give up, how much they needed to strike back at once, he gradually became conscious of a patch of the heavens visible through the window beyond the upheld newspaper and of an elongated white cloud being tugged across the sky in jerks, as if something had gone wrong with the camera or the projector so that what should have flowed together came as separate illuminations bounded before and after by darkness.

CHAPTER
FIFTY-SIX

As Meldrum was told the story, Craig Venlaw's meeting with Mrs Halliday was the product of chance, or as Venlaw put it, "It was meant to be."

At twenty-six, he was two years older than his sister Sandra. Like her, there was a certain air about him, a gloss to the skin, something pampered about the jowls, that indicated a comfortable childhood. It would have been a mistake, though, to underestimate him physically. When he was at school, his father, a dentist with a large private practice, had been heard to boast, "At the parents' night, old Gavin Sprott told me, Craig's a fine rugby player, a chip off the old block in fact. You were a mean little bastard too." In the interim, he had put on a foot so that he stood now at six foot three, an impressive figure as he ushered one or another client from drawing room to dining room, pointing out the detail of a cornice or the reminiscence of Sir William Chambers in the curve of a stairwell, so effectively that the more impressionable occasionally felt as if he was conferring a privilege rather than the chance to pay through the nose for a New Town home with a suspect roof.

He had two motives for seeking out his sister. His father had just confessed how much Sandra had been given of her inheritance in the last two years; and alarmed him with news of the size of the sum she was now asking for — all the more alarming since, knowing his father found it hard to refuse his little girl anything, she was very likely to get it. This was a motive the world could understand and sympathise with: the good son riding out to protect the family fortune. The truth was that he hardly cared since, through some accidental throwback in his genes, money mattered a good deal less to him than he was required by convention to pretend. He did, on the other hand, care about his sister more intensely than he had ever been able to admit. What had begun as a childish alliance in the face of their parents' unhappiness had deepened on his side into a crippling obsession, almost it seemed in proportion as his sister grew out of any need for his support. He had gone to see her in various digs while she was at university, flirting with her flatmates until he could be alone with her. Then when she had gone to do her teacher training, she had evaded him for a time, so that it was only yesterday after going to the College to try to discover which school she was now teaching in that he had found an address for her. Any hesitation he might have felt had disappeared with his father's confession. With the money as a pretext, he had a reason anyone would understand for needing to seek her out again.

The street didn't surprise him, it was one of those Edinburgh streets which has largely given over its flats to be shared by students and nurses and young teachers. The stair was what he expected, a little tawdry since the occupants of the shared flats were careless about getting it cleaned and indifferent to the need for repairs. What surprised him was the man who opened the door. He'd got his information from one of the lecturers at the College, a man called David Lawrence, who'd given a maliciously full description of the colleague he suspected of sleeping with Sandra, and so he'd expected a younger man, a softer man, not this hard face regarding him unsmilingly.

"Colin Halliday?" he asked without conviction.

"Who wants to know?"

"I'm Sandra Venlaw's brother."

"Should that mean something to me?"

At the tone of indifference, something hardened in him. "Let me in, and we can talk about that."

The man studied him unblinkingly for a long moment. At last he smiled and said, "If it means that much to you," opening the door wider as he stepped back. When he smiled, he looked younger.

As he described it later, Craig Venlaw was already tense with a sense of something badly wrong as he followed the man along the corridor and into a large shabbily furnished room. Although the room was cold, the sash windows were pushed up, admitting the noise of traffic from the street below.

"Talk then," the man said.

"It was Colin Halliday I wanted to talk to. Are you —?"

"Say I am."

"Is my sister here?"

"If she was, would she want to see you?"

"Of course she bloody would." Venlaw felt his muscles tighten, in his biceps, across his shoulders, in the swell of his thick neck. "Is she or isn't she?"

"Are you a fighting man?"

"Who's talking about fighting? I just want to talk to my sister."

"The difficulty is I never heard Sandra talk about having a brother." With an air of conceding a point, he added, "I knew she had a father."

"Let me tell you something about her father," Venlaw said. "He's given her all the money she's going to get. There isn't any more."

"Should I care about that?"

"Somebody's been bleeding her white."

"Would that be me?"

Something about the man told Venlaw, yes, it could have been. A woman would be attracted by his height; by the impression of tightly wound strength, the flat belly; by the face too, more ugly than handsome but full of confidence. Most women would be attracted by that physical confidence and a few like his sister by something else, an impression of danger. He knew that she longed for romance in her life, to find an escape from routine, and how could there be romance without danger?

"Is she here?"

"She's never been here."

"But you've just said that you know her."

"I know dozens of people. I don't live with them. You wanted to talk. I've talked to you. Time to go."

As Venlaw hesitated, reluctant to give up, he heard the sound of a toilet being flushed somewhere in the flat. Someone else was here. Sandra? He glanced towards the door.

"Don't even think of it," the man said.

"Someone else is here."

"No one you'd be interested in. Be sensible. I'm sorry if you're worried about her, but your sister isn't here. She hasn't ever been here."

It was said quietly and so reasonably that Venlaw saw he was behaving badly, and with the thought felt his resolution draining away.

When he spoke it was almost plaintively. "I went to the school where she teaches, but she's been off and hasn't been in touch with them to say why. I'm afraid something may have happened to her."

"How long has she been off?"

"A few days."

He didn't need the slight raising of an eyebrow, the faintest of smiles, to tell him he was over-reacting. With that, there was nothing for it but to give in and leave.

"You've no idea where she is?"

"If I had, I'd tell you. I admire a brother who wants to look after his sister. But I'm sure everything will be all right."

He'd had his back to the door all this time, but now as he turned to beat his retreat he saw the print hanging on the wall to the left of it. It presented a tangle of pastel shades slashed across with bright lines. It was called *Highland Fence*. There was a label on the back giving details of the artist. He knew this since he had given the print, number eight in a limited edition of forty, to his sister for her sixteenth birthday.

"Sandra!"

The word came out of him in a great bellow and he took a long step towards the door. In the same instant, however, a hand gripped him by the neck and brought him to a halt. The pain of that grip held him from even the thought of struggling. He hung from it like a child, and knew a strength far beyond his own.

"You should have gone when you'd the chance," the voice said, its breath warm in his ear.

Just then, two things happened. The door opened and a young man, naked except for a towel thrown over his shoulder, stared at them open mouthed.

And the doorbell rang.

With a convulsive effort, Venlaw tore himself free, burst past the young man throwing him to the side and ran to the front door, expecting every moment to be seized again in that awful grip. On the landing, an elderly woman had her hand raised to press the bell again. With a kind of sob, Venlaw caught her by the upraised hand and bore her with him down the stairs and into the street.

And this was how he and Mrs Halliday met.

CHAPTER
FIFTY-SEVEN

"It was her who told me about the murder and about you," Venlaw said. "Once she'd calmed down that is. I'd given her a hell of a fright. We sat in a café and went through a pot of tea. You know what upset her most?"

Meldrum shook his head. He was behind the desk in his office with McGuigan seated to one side.

"She's convinced the young man I saw in the flat was her son Colin. The idea of him being naked got her into a terrible state." As if by some bodily habit from his normal self, a smile tugged at the corner of his lips. "She kept saying, 'But he teaches religion.' She thinks he's been avoiding her, not answering the door or coming to see her."

"Did you know Shona Flett?" McGuigan asked.

"When Mrs Halliday said she'd been murdered that was the first I'd ever heard of her. But when I was told she as well as my sister had been a student of Colin Halliday's I thought I'd better come and see you."

An outburst of laughter came from the corridor. When Venlaw looked startled, McGuigan explained, "They caught the young thugs who killed the asylum seeker the other day. Can't blame them for celebrating a result."

"No," Venlaw said dully.

"You did the right thing coming to see us," Meldrum said.

"Do *you* think the naked guy was Colin Halliday?"

Meldrum hesitated, but more out of an ingrained reluctance to give out information than anything else. "It seems not unlikely," he admitted grudgingly.

"In that case," Venlaw asked, "who was the other one?"

"From your description, we could make a reasonable guess."

"What are you going to do about it?"

"If it's who we think it is, he had every right to be in the flat. He owns it."

"His name's Antony Crowe. He inherited the flat from Shona Flett," added McGuigan, who believed in stirring a pond to see what might surface.

"The girl who was murdered?"

"Yes."

Venlaw sat digesting this. At last, he surprised them by groaning, "What's happened to my sister? If this Shona Flett gave him her flat, maybe that's why Sandra needed money. Maybe she's been giving it to him." Unanswered, he hurried on, "I'm no coward. I've even been in fights believe it or not. But I was frightened. That man frightened me. Will you come back with me and search the flat?"

"I'm sorry," Meldrum said, "we'd need a warrant to do that, and there aren't any grounds for us to be given one."

274

"He attacked me. I'm making a formal complaint. I thought he was going to — I was in fear for my life."

"We have your statement, and we'll follow it up. We'll interview him. But it'll be your word against his, I'm afraid."

"Look!" Venlaw pulled his collar clear of his neck and bent his head. The marks on his skin were turning a livid yellow. "That's where he gripped me."

"It might be worse than your word against his," McGuigan said. "Chances are Halliday will back him up in whatever story he tells."

"We'll look for your sister," Meldrum said. "I can only promise we'll do our best."

Venlaw looked at them, and his eyes shone as if with unshed tears.

"I don't know what to do," he said.

The three men sat in silence.

CHAPTER
FIFTY-EIGHT

"Something not right there," McGuigan said. "He looked ready to start greeting. Did you see his eyes?"

"He was worried about his sister."

"I suppose. But when he came in at first, it was all about money. She'd been after her father for money. Blah blah blah. She could wrap her father round her wee finger. There was something fishy going on. But the hard man act didn't last long. *He* didn't care about the money."

"A lot of men don't like to show emotion. She was his sister."

"Exactly. Just his sister. Did you ever carry a picture of your sister round in your wallet? You tell him it would be useful to have a photograph, and I've got one here, he says. Just like that. It's not right."

It was as eloquent as Meldrum had heard McGuigan being for a long time. He wondered what it was about Venlaw that had got under the sergeant's skin.

"Anyway, him having it saves us time."

"Not," McGuigan said gloomily, "that it'll do us much good. If Halliday's neighbours couldn't recognise a beauty like Keeley Robertson, why should they recognise this one?"

But one of them did. The elderly man on the ground floor had come to the door in his carpet slippers as he had done when interviewed about Keeley Robertson. This time, however, he responded at once to the photograph they showed him.

"She was one of them. I'd swear it on a stack of Bibles, if you want."

"How can you be so sure?"

"She liked cats, that's why. I opened the door one time to let Rusty in, and she was crouched down rubbing him behind the ears. We talked for a bit. She was a real cat lover. And I saw her again a couple of times — when Rusty had been out." His smile showed a ragged line of yellow teeth. "Which he is a lot. Got a better social life than I have."

From his place stretched out by the heat of the fire, Rusty held Meldrum's gaze for a moment before wincing and glancing aside.

CHAPTER
FIFTY-NINE

"Antony isn't here," Bridget O'Neill said, blocking the doorway.

Once again, Meldrum was baffled by the spectacle she presented. She was wearing a dressing gown, soiled down the front with traces of old meals. Her dirty yellow hair stood up as if unbrushed for days. The skin around her eyes had the seamed lines cut into the flesh of the heavy smoker. He could see no trace in her of the woman who had been the great love of Michael Thorne's life.

"When will he be back?"

"He won't be. He's staying in town for a few days." With a kind of defiance, an attempt at hauteur, she said, "He owns a flat in town, you know."

"We know. He isn't there or, if he is, he's not answering the door."

"He'll have gone out for a paper or a drink. Something like that."

"Maybe," Meldrum said. It made perfect sense, and yet both McGuigan and he, as they beat a tattoo on the door of Halliday's flat, had shared a strong feeling that their man had already decamped.

"Did he say when to expect him back?" McGuigan asked.

"He's not a child. He doesn't have to account for himself to me."

"When he comes back, tell him it would be stupid not to come and talk to us," Meldrum said.

"What's he done?" she asked in sharp alarm, before closing her lips tightly as if to restrain the words which had escaped.

McGuigan said, "Just tell him to come and see us. Otherwise we'll be looking for him."

On impulse, Meldrum asked, "Do you want to talk out here? We'd be better inside."

At this, he was conscious of McGuigan, already half turned away, jerking his head round to give him a hard glance. If there had been a chance to explain, or if he'd felt any inclination to do so, Meldrum might have said the only end to this case would lie not in forensics or even the accumulation of detail by dogged police work but in finding some way to use Crowe's nature against him. It was a conviction he'd been edging towards since the night Crowe came to his flat; but that was a visit he intended to keep to himself.

Reluctantly she led them into the front room.

"What have you got to tell me?" she asked.

"Isn't it the other way round?" Meldrum wondered. "You realise the kind of trouble you would be in if you've been telling lies?"

"I haven't told any lies!"

"Not about the night the young woman Shona Flett was killed? I never met her, but I've seen her photograph. A nice looking woman — she's laughing in the photograph — someone you couldn't help liking, I'd guess. And, of course, I saw the body. It had been cut about. He'd made a mess of her."

"*He* — what does that mean? Who are you talking about?"

"The man who killed her. Did we say the body had been mutilated very badly? It's not something I like to talk about, but he'd cut her on both breasts and between the legs. It made me wonder if he was sane. Sometimes you can't tell. A man can appear perfectly normal. Talk about everyday things and even make jokes. Meeting him you might think he was a good husband or a good son. But inside there's something gone badly wrong. He's twisted inside."

McGuigan cleared his throat and shifted his weight uneasily.

"You've no right to talk to me like this." Although the woman's voice trembled uncontrollably, strangely just for an instant as she held herself very erect as if in defiance, Meldrum had a glimpse of the woman she must once have been.

"If you knew someone had done a thing like that," Meldrum went on, "it would be wrong to tell lies for him. Wrong to claim he'd been at home when he wasn't. If you went into court and told a lie like that — if it got to court — the judge would call it perjury. You can go to jail for perjury. If the case is serious that is." He paused and shook his head. "There isn't anything more serious than murder."

"I want you to leave now," Bridget O'Neill said.

280

No sooner were the words out of her mouth than McGuigan was opening the door into the hall.

As they made their way to the front door, Meldrum said, "The night your partner died — do you want to claim that you phoned your son to tell him? Or do you want to change your mind? Maybe there's something else you want to tell us?"

She brushed past him and opened the outside door.

"I don't remember," she said. "It — it was a long time ago."

"When you see your son, tell him I've been here and that we had a little chat about perjury."

As she stared at him, her lips began to tremble. After a moment, she closed the door, not with a bang as might have been expected, but gently as if it might shatter in her hand.

Going back to the car, McGuigan strode ahead.

They were almost back into the city before he sighed and asked, "What was all that about?" And went on without waiting for a reply, "I'm telling you straight, I've just about had enough."

CHAPTER
SIXTY

Marie tried to pretend she didn't see him watching her. The bar of the hotel was busy and she had no idea how long he had been there. It was a relief when a man in a blue suit tight across the belly bought her a drink and asked if he could join her. Not long after he'd concluded, "You're a good listener," it was clear to both of them that he was interested in buying what she had to sell.

"I'm staying here," he said at last. "Nice room. You'll like it."

She smiled and refrained from saying how long it had been since anything in a room like that could surprise or please her.

"One thing though. I'll have to go to a place first. I'd hate to have an accident in the lift."

She smiled agreeably and watched him set off a little unsteadily for the toilet. A weak bladder, she thought, probably meant he wouldn't last long in bed. As she gathered her bag, she noticed with relief that the man who'd been watching her was no longer there.

Just as she had begun to get uneasy about the time that had elapsed, she felt a light touch on her shoulder.

"Thought you were lost," she said, and broke off as she looked up into the face of the man who had been watching her.

"Jack," she said.

Crowe smiled at the name. Was that what he'd called himself? Why not John? John must be the name that popped into most heads. *What's your name, dear? John.* Maybe that's why the girls called clients Johns. Everybody gave a false name to whores. He would have thought of himself as being more original.

"Let's go," he said, smiling down at her.

"I can't." She tried to control her breathing. "I'm waiting for somebody."

"Don't worry about it. He won't be coming back."

"But —" She had been watching all the time. How could he have gone without her seeing him? Could he still be in the toilet?

She felt his fingers fold around her arm; saw that his knuckles were flecked with dots of blood. At his urging, she got to her feet. If she had looked back as they left, she would have seen a sudden flurry of activity around the entrance to the toilets.

In the taxi, she stared at the back of the driver's head. All the girls knew Billy. She could appeal to him for help, refuse to get out of the taxi. It was a measure of her fear that she would even consider doing that. It was such a stupid idea. Even if he'd been thirty years younger, Billy had never been a knight in shining armour.

Beside her, watching the street lights play over the dim interior, Crowe's nostrils spread like those of a cat patting a mouse with a shielded paw.

What has she to be afraid of? he thought; and though dimly a memory stirred of the night he had beaten her, it seemed nothing compared to the car wreck of his own life. Since his mother had told him of her ordeal with Meldrum, he had understood that everything was about to unravel. He had spent time in jail and had the scars of wardens' boots to prove it. There was no way he would ever go back.

As she went ahead of him up the stairs, he watched her arse sway from side to side. Like cats in a sack, he thought. She can't help doing it, he decided, though he suspected sex was the last thing in the world she cared about at that moment. If he leaned forward, he could pull down those tight pants and sink his teeth into the white flesh of her rump. In the hotel bar, he'd sat for an hour keeping an eye on her, wanting to lust after her, sometimes almost fooling himself that he did, sometimes so lost in his anger that he was blind to her although his eyes didn't move.

When she put on the light, the room disgusted him with its faint smell of unwashed bodies and the bucket under the table with a used condom draped over the edge.

She turned and slipped her jacket from her shoulders, letting it lie where it fell on the floor. "We'd be more comfortable next door." She had no strategy but getting him into bed and hoping that he would go afterwards.

He went to the door and peered into the bedroom. Turning, he shoved her aside as he went back into the first room and sat down in the easy chair that sat beside the gas fire. As she watched, he turned it on and lit the bars with a match from the box. When he'd done that, he dropped the spent match among the others that littered the hearth.

"Don't be in such a hurry. Have you anything to drink?"

"There's beer."

"You can do better than that."

He heard her opening cupboards in the kitchen. When she came back, she was carrying a tumbler with whisky in it. He sipped and made a face.

"Get one for yourself." He handed her the tumbler. "And put something in this piss. Ice, if you've got any."

This time she had two tumblers. She handed him the one with the ice, the other was full of a dark liquid.

"What's that?"

"Whisky and coke."

"They deserve one another." He took another sip. "That's better. Ice locks in the flavour, so that all you can taste is alcohol. Did you know that?"

She shook her head. He saw that her hand was trembling so that the liquid in the glass washed back and forward. Deliberately then, as an exercise, he set out to soothe her fears. He spoke softly, his voice almost a murmur, smiled at the least opportunity and laughed once as if pleasantly surprised by something she said. It amused him to see how easily it worked, how the fear her body had been taught by him even worked to undermine any resistance, as if she was afraid to allow herself to be suspicious or to be impatient as she would normally have been with a client. If he wanted to talk, then perhaps she must have thought it would all end well. When he insisted on going into the kitchen to refill their glasses, putting this time a full measure of whisky into her glass, she made no resistance.

"Tell me more," he said, once he had coaxed her into talking.

"After my father died, we had to bring ourselves up. My mother had died in childbirth with my sister Noleen. My oldest brother was only eighteen. It's a wonder the social wasn't round putting us in Homes. But we rubbed along. It wasn't bad. We had fun. My brothers Danny and Phil and Francis had one good coat among them. On a Saturday they'd take turns to wear it, when they were courting or whatever. Monday it would go back into the pawnshop. Danny had a nice girlfriend, nice family, lived in a nice house. He turned up at her door this Saturday and her father said to him, Where's your coat, Danny? You can't go out in just your jacket. It's perishing out. Oh, Danny says without thinking, we've lost the ticket!"

"Stupid bastard!" Crowe laughed, sinking deeper in his chair and nursing the glass on his stomach.

"Everybody that was working gave their paypacket to my sister Elsie. She ran the house because she was the oldest girl. And she was only twelve!"

"What age were you?"

"Four when my father died. I remember there was an old woman in the close that would look in sometimes to see how we were getting on. I'd heard them talking about her. Blah blah blah, they said. She'll sit and talk at us — blah blah blah. So this time, when she was in and there was a bit of a pause, I looked up at her and said, When are you going to give us your blah! I got some stick for that, but I didn't mean any harm. I'd no idea what it meant."

He laughed again. "Big family, it must have been."

"God, yes. The boys went to the army, though, or down south for work." She sighed. "Everything changed."

"Roman Catholics, were you?"

She nodded and then looked wary as if unsure how he would take that.

"My father was a priest," he said. As she stared in surprise, he burst into laughter.

Laughing, she said, "That's a new one."

He struggled up in the chair and put his finger to his lips. "I'm going to tell you a secret," he said.

She smiled in response, and for a time the smile stayed on her face as if forgotten. As he went on with perfect seriousness, however, it slowly faded.

"This is something I first heard about when I was in the army. You know what the first Gulf War was? I'll tell you. We were in Iraq and that's where I met a man, not a white man, who told me about the third secret of Fatima. You know about the miracle at Fatima?"

"The Virgin Mary appeared to some children. When I was a bairn, I wondered what that must have been like for them."

"She told them three secrets. Two were about Russia spreading communism and then collapsing. But the third was never revealed. This guy I met claimed to know it, though. Fatima wasn't just a town in Portugal he told me. It was the name of the favourite daughter of the prophet Mohammed. But — not many white people know this — in Islam they admire the Virgin Mary even more than Fatima. That's something the Muslims and us Catholics have in common. All of us love and venerate the Virgin. What do you make of that?"

"I never knew." She was no longer smiling.

"And another thing. Protestants used to believe in the Devil, but they don't now, not any more. The Muslims are like us, though, they still believe in Him. Iblis is their name for the Devil. When Mohammed on his travels came to an unfamiliar bit of country, he'd say a special prayer just in case the shaidans were there. Shaidans is their name for what we call demons."

She looked uncertain.

"Isn't it true a priest can do an exorcism?" he asked impatiently. "Well, then, what do you think he's exorcising? So there's another way we're the same. Do you like Muslims?"

"Not much," she said. "If I was being honest."

"All right in the way of business, eh?"

"I suppose."

"A lot of people don't like them. Women with their faces covered up — how can you tell what they're thinking? It's not just the men who carry bombs. John Paul II tried to make friends with the Muslims, though. He was the first Pope ever to preach in a mosque. Hard to tell who was kidding who, eh? The Pope in a mosque."

288

She looked at him uneasily. "Is that true?"

"Would I lie to you? He did it in 2001. In the Umayyad Mosque in Damascus."

"You know a lot about all this stuff," she said, suitably admiring.

"I know the third secret of Fatima," he said. "This guy in Iraq told me, and years later an old priest in Edinburgh confirmed it. Want me to tell you it?"

"Would that be all right?"

"In a minute." Going into the kitchen, he refilled their glasses. When he handed one to her, he held on to it. She looked up startled. "But, if I tell you," he said quietly, "you'll become one of us."

"What do you mean?"

"There are two sides," he said. "Once you know the secret, you'll have to join the right side. Shall I tell you?"

He released her glass, and pushed the chair he'd been sitting in closer to hers, so close their knees touched. He leaned forward.

"The third secret of Fatima is that the Catholics and the Muslims are going to get together. Together they could rule the world."

He sat back and waited. She looked at him blank-faced.

"Did you expect something more exciting?"

She started to say something, stopped and tried again. "Would the Pope do that?" she asked carefully.

"You're a simple woman," he said, "but that's not a simple question. The last Pope wanted to make friends with Islam. But the new one, Benedict, he loves

Europe. He sees the danger that our values and way of life might be wiped out. He's said, we've gone too far with all this multiculturalism — so far it amounts to giving up what makes us what we are."

"There you are then."

"There we are," he repeated slowly as if talking to a child. "I can see what side you are going to be on."

"What side?"

"The same one as me and my friends. The same one as the old priest in Edinburgh who got himself killed." She opened her mouth and closed it again. "A holy man. There are lots of us, all over the world. Fighting to stop it happening. Working in secret because we have no choice. That's what I've taught some people. I call them my disciples."

"But if the Pope doesn't want it!"

"Popes have been killed."

She crossed herself and shrank back as his knees pressed hers.

After a moment of silence, he sat back and smiled.

"You know what a disciple is, don't you? A disciple is someone who will believe whatever you tell them. You're not a disciple."

"Sorry?"

"You don't believe any of this, do you?" he said impatiently.

"It's not something I'd know about."

"Because you're not clever. Right?"

"Nobody ever called me clever." She tried a smile.

"Isn't it strange what clever people will believe? I mean really clever people. It never ceases to amaze me.

Clever fools, eh? And here you are just a simple woman, but clever enough to see through this rigmarole. Don't tell me you're not. That would irritate me. Be honest. I admire honesty."

She hung between possibilities, eyes as wide as a rabbit in the stare of a stoat.

"Compared to someone like you, I'm stupid."

"No argument there. But all that stuff about the papes and the towel heads getting together, that's nonsense, isn't it? Nobody would be stupid enough to swallow that, would they?"

"It's hard to believe," she said tentatively.

"Hard to believe," he mimicked her. "It's worse than that. *It's a load of shite.*"

With that he began to laugh so freely and — what had been his word? — so honestly that she started to smile.

"What is it?" he gasped, shoulders heaving. "Tell me. What is it?"

"A load of shite," she said and found herself laughing with him.

Their mingled laughter made a pleasant sound. He didn't stop laughing even when he leaned forward and punched her in the face.

"Demons," he said, "you can believe in demons."

The first blow broke her nose.

CHAPTER
SIXTY-ONE

Within hours of the body of Marie being found by the only sister who still kept in touch with her, there was little doubt as to who had killed her. There was a DNA match (spittle in one case, urine in the other) between her killer and the assailant who'd beaten the man in the blue suit to a pulp and left him on the floor of the hotel toilet. Since the assailant had already been identified by one of the waiters and two of Marie's colleagues who'd been keeping a jealous eye on proceedings, Antony Crowe was being sought on suspicion of murder before the day was out.

When detectives got no answer at the flat where Colin Halliday stayed in Marchmont, a locksmith was called who gave them entry. Dirty plates in the sink bore traces of food fresh enough to suggest the place had been occupied within the last few days. Examined at leisure, the evidence of clothes and sheets suggested male and female occupancy. There was nothing, however, after the most careful inspection, to give a hint as to where those occupants had gone. Using the DNA sample that they now knew to be Crowe's confirmed that he had eaten in the flat and used the bed for sex of some kind in the room that must have been Colin Halliday's.

"All vanished into thin air," Meldrum summed up at the end of the second day. "Colin Halliday hasn't been back to the College. Let's assume the two women lived there with him and Shona Flett. Sandra Venlaw hasn't been back to work, and Keeley Robertson has stopped attending classes. Parents don't know where they are. Nothing from friends. In fact, both of them seem to have cut themselves off from friends over the last year. As for Crowe . . ."

As for Crowe, they'd gone to the cottage where at first the mother had assumed they had come back to check on the alibi she'd given her son for the night of Shona Flett's murder. Before they could explain why they were there, "Don't waste your time," she'd told them. "He was with me that night and the night Peter got killed outside the pub. It's God's truth and I won't change my mind. You should stop harassing him. He wouldn't hurt a fly. I'm his mother. Do you think I wouldn't know?"

"What about the night before last?" McGuigan had asked.

After they'd explained to her what a warrant was, she followed them from room to room. Crowe wasn't there, but Meldrum examined his room with interest. Unlike the rest of the house, it was neat, the bed made up military style with the corners squared away and the top covering taut. On a table beside it, there was a water jug with a tumbler upside down on top of it. A shelf for books had been constructed in one corner out of a plank of wood set on three stacks of bricks. At one end it had *A History of the Arab Peoples*, *Hitler's Pope*, *A Dictionary of Saints*, Celtic Mythology; the rest of the space was taken up by paperbacks, to which Meldrum paid no attention after establishing that they all seemed to be novels. A wardrobe held two suits, one brown, one blue, both of good quality. The shoes ranged on the floor underneath were also expensive, as was the collection of shirts in the drawer. According to the mother, there wasn't a photograph of him in the house; and she had never seen one of him.

The last thing she said to them was, "What has he done this time?"

A question to which, in the way of policemen, they had taken care not to provide an answer.

"So much for Crowe," Meldrum said to the assembled team. "It's been splashed in the papers this morning. No one's come forward yet. So now we go back and talk again to everyone. Sharkey'll do the army records. Petrie and Lang get the names of the two men who went to prison with him for the armed robbery charge. Find them and see if either of them has been in touch with him since."

It was the next day before Meldrum and McGuigan paid a second call on Lester Peters, the lawyer who had handled Shona Flett's will in which she'd named Antony Crowe as her beneficiary.

"I'm so glad you're here," the lawyer said, a statement improbable enough to put Meldrum on the alert.

"Why would that be?"

"If you hadn't turned up, I was going to come and see you." He reached into the briefcase sitting on the floor at the side of his desk and pulled out a copy of that morning's *Scotsman*. "They didn't have a photograph of him, but it is the same Antony Crowe?"

"Shona Flett's heir?" Meldrum nodded. "That's the one."

"I couldn't help hoping it wasn't, but I knew it had to be. And you're searching for him?"

"To help with our enquries."

"What does that mean?"

"What it says. So why were you going to come and see me?"

Peters folded the paper and slid it back into the briefcase. As he did so, he said, "It *was* him who killed this prostitute?" Taking silence as consent, he visibly made up his mind to begin. "That will I drew up for Miss Flett. It wasn't the first piece of business I'd done for her."

"What was the other business?" Meldrum asked.

In the same moment, McGuigan said, "Was Crowe involved?"

"It happened six months before the will was drawn up. Shona Flett sold Crowe a house. Even then, I wasn't entirely happy about it. I wasn't persuaded that money had really changed hands. But she owned the house all right. No problem with the searches, all that side of it was straightforward."

"It would have helped if you'd told us this before."

"I didn't see that it would help to bring it up. There is such a thing as client confidentiality. But now, you're looking for him." He threw up his hands. "I have a duty to help. One more thing! It's a remote property. I could imagine someone might go there to hide."

CHAPTER
SIXTY-TWO

When the old woman tried to open her eyes, her lids were gummed together so that it took an effort before she made out the shape of a man seated opposite her, and then recognised him as her son. He was studying her with an expression she couldn't read. She had no idea how long he had been sitting there.

Struggling up in the chair, she said, "The police have been here. They went into your room."

"It doesn't matter."

"What have you done?"

He held up his hands with the backs turned towards her. When she stared uncomprehendingly, he leaned forward until she could make out the swollen and broken knuckles.

"You've hurt yourself."

"Do you want to kiss it better?"

"What?" The request bewildered her.

"Isn't that what mothers do? Isn't that what a mummy would do?"

"You're a grown man, not a wee boy."

He ran his tongue across the back of his right hand, and then put a knuckle in his mouth. When he held it up again, she could see the wet smear where he'd chewed off a scab of blood.

"Did you hurt somebody?"

"You could say that. There wasn't much of her face left."

"A woman? For God's sake, why would you hit a woman?"

"Well," he said slowly as if working it out, "everything is over for me. And she happened to be there."

"You shouldn't have hit a woman."

"It was probably a mistake. But it was fun at the time."

"My father said only a coward would hit a woman."

"That would be grandpa," he said, chewing on his knuckles. "Christ, when I think of the family life I've missed."

She put her hands on the arms and hitched herself to the edge of the chair.

"Stay where you are," he said.

She sank back.

"The police have already been looking for you. It's not safe. You can't stay here."

"You want me to go?"

"I'm just saying, if it's not safe . . . It's you I'm thinking about."

"I thought you might be frightened."

She shook her head. "You wouldn't hurt your mother."

"Because you looked after me when I was wee?"

"I wanted to," the old woman said.

"Too late now."

But you came to find me, she thought, staring at him, trying to understand him. Giving it up at last as beyond her, she said, "They could be back any time looking for you. You can't stay here."

"Where do you think I should go?"

"Where were you before you came here? Have you nobody could put you up? Somebody in London? A place as big as that, how would they find you there?"

"Trust a mother's heart," Crowe said. "I can see you're trying to help. But, you know, I don't think there's anywhere would hide me now."

"You could do it. Don't tell me you couldn't hide. You think I don't know how special you are?"

"You've no idea how special I am. Like Jesus, I have disciples."

"You shouldn't talk like that."

"Before Gethsemane, you think Jesus couldn't have found a place to hide? But when it came to the bit, he didn't want to. Away to fuck with it, he said, I can't be bothered."

That's not right, save the world, what His Father wanted, let this cup pass from me, died for us. It was all there churning in her head, but the words wouldn't come. How young had she been when Michael Thorne took her to the Kelvin Hall for that Billy Graham rally? A Protestant thing. We shouldn't be here, she'd told him. But there had been a singer called George Beverly Shea, a lovely voice, like Bing Crosby. And then Graham, tall and earnest, big shovel hands on him like a boy off the farm, talking about how little time we were given on earth to choose between evil and everlasting life. And at the end, she'd started to get up out of her seat, and would have gone down to be saved if Michael Thorne hadn't laughed and put his hand on her arm to hold her still.

"Have you gone to sleep? What's wrong with you?"

"Christ died for our sins."

"When was the last time you were at mass?"

"I'll go now and pray for you."

He spat a little blood out of his mouth on to the carpet.

"Those police that came. The tall man was one of them?"

She nodded.

"He'll be back to see you soon."

"What for?"

What are you going to do would make them come back? She was afraid to ask.

"He's not like the others. I wish I could have talked more to him. When he comes, get him by himself. Just him on his own. Tell him you have a message for him from me. Tell him, my son had disciples who believed everything he told them. Tell him, when my only son left me he went off to prove their faith. Can you remember that?"

"Are you saying these things to punish me?"

He blinked at her as if in surprise. "You're just the messenger. All you have to do is remember."

Feeling herself denied, she cried out on a whiteness of anger like youth renewed, "I'm your mother and you can't forgive me for not keeping you."

"I can't forgive you for having me," Crowe said softly. "All it would have taken was a knitting needle up inside you."

CHAPTER
SIXTY-THREE

Sandra Venlaw, who had been cold for days, felt her spirit unclench as she sat on the stone wall at the bottom of the garden soaking up the gift of a late summer sun. Eyes closed, she luxuriated like a cat as its warmth stroked her cheeks and shoulders. She listened lazily to the whirring of crickets in the grass and a blackbird threading its melody through the gentle remonstrance of ewes in the field. At the sound of the back door opening, she squinted one eye open and was sorry to see Keeley Robertson picking her way towards her. It was snobbish to feel superior; but at least it wasn't the vulgarity of social or money superiority. To be an intellectual snob had always seemed to her altogether more acceptable. Oddly enough, when they had wrapped themselves in the cloaks of Grania and Emer, she hadn't felt the younger woman's inferiority of intellect so keenly. Then instead she had been envious of her beauty and felt her own energy dulling in contrast to the vibrant life that shone from that mane of red hair.

"I've been watching you," Keeley said.

With a sigh, Sandra opened both eyes. "Nothing to see," she said.

"You were smiling."

"You make it sound like an accusation."

"What?"

"It isn't a sin. Smiling."

"What can you find to smile about?"

"Do you really want to know? I was remembering something my father told me. He was a deacon in the Episcopal Church when we lived in Stirlingshire. They used a long bag on a stick to take up the collection. 'Sometimes,' he told me, 'there is less in it when it comes back!'"

"Was that all?"

"It came into my head for some reason."

The young woman slumped down beside her on the wall. She might have waited to be asked, Sandra thought, unreasonably irritated.

"When do you think they will be back? Colin was so strange."

"From their mysterious errand," Sandra murmured. "But then everything Antony does is mysterious."

Keeley gave a little sound that made Sandra turn to look at her. She's like a kitten going to be sick, she thought unkindly.

"I can't get used to calling him that."

"It's his name. And, as he says, there's no point in secrecy any more. Our enemies know all they need to know about us."

There was a long silence. In a voice so soft that Sandra wondered if she had misheard, the younger woman asked, "Do you believe in them?"

Slumped forward with her head down, the girl's face was veiled by the curtain of hair. Sandra twisted round to look at her. "People have died," she said. "This isn't the time to stop believing."

"I was the one who never doubted. I believed everything the Convenor told us."

"Antony." As she said his name, she saw his face as it had smiled down on her that first night when, with his seed newly implanted in her, he had told her of the Third Secret of Fatima. Hard to read that expression, even now she had no way of interpreting his smile, and yet almost without words he had made her understand that this secret would shape the remainder of her life.

"I thought of myself as more faithful than Colin," Keeley said. "Certainly, more than you. I don't know if I could make you understand how proud that made me."

"I had an idea. So what's changed?"

"The name was wrong — the man we killed — Nicholas Aaron wasn't an Arab name. And then last night I couldn't sleep. Every time I shut my eyes —"

Before she could stop herself, Sandra said bitterly, "Antony was fucking you again."

"*What? What? What?*"

Oh God, don't let her be hysterical. "Every time you shut your eyes . . .?" she asked soothingly.

"I saw Colin bending over the old man lying on the floor. And lying in the dark it seemed there was so much blood, far more than there really was . . . Sandra?"

"Yes?"

304

"What's going to happen to us?"

Sandra closed her eyes again. It was strange how even now she could find pleasure in the touch of the sun on her cheek. She wondered if such moments could still find the very old or the terminally ill and descend on them like an animal blessing in the midst of the greyness and prevailing misery. As she felt a tentative touch upon her arm, her own despair, self-contempt and anger drained away.

Moved by pity for all of them, the living and the dead, all the victims, she told poor Emer, "Since we're damned, it really doesn't matter any more."

CHAPTER
SIXTY-FOUR

For once Meldrum was glad to be driven. In shock as they came down from the hills, he pressed his hands together to hide their trembling from McGuigan. What motive could there be for what they had seen? But then what motive would explain Charles Manson, or his followers who had butchered some pregnant actress like an animal? Explain it by Manson's lust for power and their need for submission? Explain it by his anger against his life in the world? If everything else failed, listen to the minister from the long ago childhood pulpit and call it evil? How could a policeman settle for that?

There were more obvious things waiting to be done, but Meldrum set them all aside, since there was only one place he wanted to go. As he stood waiting with McGuigan, the curious eye of the camera on the factory wall passed over them as it checked back and forth.

"No one in," McGuigan said.

He sounded relieved, as if with the prospect of speaking to the other relatives he'd already wearied of the thankless task ahead.

"I doubt she'll go out much," Meldrum said.

306

He went along the front of the cottage, glancing in at the windows, and looked down the path at the side. It was overgrown with weeds and littered with half-filled plastic sacks sat against the wall. Behind the cottage what had once been a lawn was knee-high in wild grass. The back door resisted for a moment and then gave as if only the damp that had swollen the wood frame had held it shut.

"Now what?" McGuigan asked at his back.

Without answering he pushed until he could see into a kitchen with an iron range for cooking and a pulley draped with dishcloths dangling from the ceiling. The figure of a woman sat at the table.

"Mrs O'Neill?"

"I've been waiting for you."

She didn't lift her head or look round, and the voice was no more than a dry whisper. There was so little emotion in it that he asked in confusion, "Why?"

"My son said you would come."

"Did he say why?" McGuigan asked.

When she didn't answer, Meldrum said, "I've afraid we've bad news for you."

"What has he done?"

Damned himself to hell, Meldrum thought.

"Your son is dead."

She sat so still she might not have heard.

He tried again, "At the moment, it seems as if he killed himself."

"Are you sure he's dead?"

"Yes." Surprised by the question, he could offer only the raw confirmation of the fact.

She raised her head for the first time and looked at him. "You should go back and make sure. My son pretends."

"When did he leave the house?" McGuigan asked, and getting no answer went on, "Was he carrying anything?" Met by silence, the third question came with the effect of a nervous tic. "Did he say anything to you?"

"We can come back," Meldrum said. "Have you anyone who could stay with you? We could ask a policewoman to call in, if you wanted."

"You were here before," she said at last.

"We both were," McGuigan said.

"He called you the tall man," she said to Meldrum.

"When was that?" McGuigan asked. "Before he left?"

Again she ignored him.

"Have you something to tell *me*?" Meldrum asked, unable to stop himself, and for a moment he actually believed a message had been left for him and everything would be explained.

She shook her head.

"I have nothing to say to you," she said. "Not now or ever."

CHAPTER
SIXTY-FIVE

Unable to sleep, at the end of an interminable night, Meldrum had fetched the car from its parking place in the street and taken the shore road out of Edinburgh. Within half an hour, he was pulling into the Bents at Longniddry. The tide was far out and he walked down until he could step out on the long ribbon of firm sand from which the sea had shrunk. It was a cold clear morning with not a breath of wind, and the Forth stretched out ahead in an unruffled illusion of stillness.

It had begun with the body of an old recluse and now it was over, he thought, and then reflected that the true beginning must have been years earlier when a young priest fell in love with a girl he thought would never grow old.

The dawn was so clear he could pick out separate buildings like toy models on the opposite shore. Walking by the edge of the sea had always brought him peace. Now as a man with a dog gave him a nod in passing, he was reminded of Shona Flett and how she had lain some miles along this coast like a mutilated doll among the marram grass.

It was a relief after the hot stickiness of a wakeful night to feel the air cold on his face. He hadn't had a full night's sleep since the case had ended a week earlier. After getting the address from the lawyer Lester Peters, he and McGuigan had gone up into the hills outside the city to check out the property, described as derelict, that Shona Flett had sold, or given, to Antony Crowe. Neither of them had harboured any real expectation of finding Crowe there, but as they turned off the main road onto the track that wound up the valley the clouds had gathered at the head of the pass and some premonition had darkened their mood.

By the time they came to the hillside of burned and twisted trees, they were almost relieved to be persuaded that they had taken the wrong road. Shortly afterwards, however, they had come on the grey stone house with its drawn curtains crouched under the rising slope of a field scattered with sheep. Their nerves tightened at the sight of a car parked outside.

"Somebody's here," McGuigan said.

By an unspoken agreement, he ran the car on until the house was out of sight.

As they walked back, he asked, "Want me to take the back door?"

Remembering, Meldrum could recall the quality of the silence around the beat of McGuigan's footsteps while he waited, one hand raised ready to knock. When he drummed with his fist on the front door, the silence was broken. As he paused and waited, the birds sang again. He was about to knock for a second time, when McGuigan reappeared.

"Better come and look."

What he saw through the kitchen window left no choice but to break into the house. They used a side window to keep the kitchen undisturbed, breaking the glass and reaching in to slide the catch back.

All four of them had died in the kitchen. The two women and Colin Halliday lay on the floor, thrown from their chairs by their dying struggles. Antony Crowe was slumped forward with his head resting on the table, arms thrown out and hands open as if nailed to the wood. The post-mortems identified the cause of death, the same for all four. On the table stood three bottles of grape juice. The mixture in the bottles and the dregs in each of the four glasses contained cyanide and a number of sedatives including liquid valium, a morphine derivative and chloral hydrate. Crowe's were the only fingerprints on the bottles, indicating that he must have poured the fatal drinks into each of the glasses. There was nothing to indicate that any of the others had been forced to drink. As far as the event could be reconstructed, it seemed they had sat around the table and drained their glasses voluntarily and died together.

Some time later, perhaps still in a state of shock, he had broken the practice of a lifetime and apologised to McGuigan for suspecting him of beating up the prostitute Marie. The sergeant had grunted and turned away, but not before he'd seen in his eyes contempt for such a show of weakness.

Four people had died in some kind of suicide pact and nothing made sense. One at least of them had been a murderer. It wasn't unheard of that with a single killer the motive would be a matter of pathology, never entirely to be understood. But what sane person could construct a reason for four people to kill a stranger like Nicholas Aaron?

Putting his head back, Meldrum watched a plane angle out from the airport and climb sharply before turning inland. The day before, his daughter Betty had taken a flight from Glasgow to New York. He hadn't been there to see her off. There was no way of being sure that he would ever see her again. He couldn't protect her; he couldn't protect her mother; he couldn't protect his grandson.

Nothing made sense.

An observer would have watched him diminish as he made his way along towards the end of the beach, and perhaps been surprised by what happened then. At that distance, though, there would have been no way of making sense of those arms thrown out towards the crags and steeples of the old city across the water and all its inhabitants unprotected under their Castle from personal demons and the contagion of madness shared.

As it happened, standing by the water's edge the early morning dog walker was the only other occupant of the beach, and his attention was fixed upon a tanker as it beat its way out from the firth towards the open sea.

By the time he turned his head, the moment had passed.